HEARTS IN PERIL™

Remote Danger

Katy Lee

Annie's®
AnniesFiction.com

Books in the Hearts in Peril series

... and more to come!

Library of Congress-in-Publication Data
Remote Danger / by Katy Lee
p. cm.
ISBN: 978-1-64025-794-8
I. Title
                    2023932895

AnniesFiction.com
(800) 282-6643
Hearts in Peril™
Series Creator: Shari Lohner
Series Editor: Amy Woods

10 11 12 13 14 | Printed in China | 9 8 7 6 5 4 3 2 1

1

*P*eople often associated plane crashes with conspiracy, and for the first time in his five years of flying, Kaden Phillips wondered if they were onto something. As he struggled to regain control of his small charter aircraft over a mountain peak in northern Washington, he blinked his eyes to clear away the leftover flash of light that had blinded him. A mysterious object had collided with his left wing in the darkness and left him struggling to maintain altitude. The investigators would comb through the rubble and search for a mechanical failure or blame it on the pilot. They wouldn't know that something outside the plane had taken him down.

Or had it?

Kaden wasn't sure of anything. Maybe he had dozed off and hit the tip of a tree in the dead of night. Maybe the bright light had been part of a dream. How it had happened mattered less than surviving at the moment.

He veered to his left to avoid a direct collision with a solid rock face. He had no idea whether he would clear the mountain in time, but he had to try. He noticed his reflexes felt slower and instantly checked the gauge for pressurization, which was set correctly. There could have been a leak in the fuselage, a tiny hole that would doom the flight to disaster. The smart thing was to put on his oxygen mask before full hypoxia set in—if it hadn't already. He thought he was handling the controls correctly, but if he had succumbed to hypoxia, would he even know? The mind-altering impairment would affect his judgment.

It would make him hallucinate and see things that weren't there.

Like a flashing light.

Kaden knew he had to land his plane to assess the damage, including his own well-being. In the middle of the night and in unfamiliar, mountainous terrain, the best thing he could do was find a place to bring her down safely. He wouldn't make it to Alaska without some form of repairs or even a new craft altogether. The job he'd anticipated would have to wait, at least for the time being.

The suspicion crept into his mind that someone from his family could have sabotaged his plane to keep him from the new life he was trying to build.

Now I'm being delusional.

Kaden kept an eye on the controls and his surroundings. A dark valley appeared between two peaks, and he aimed the plane's swaying nose in that direction. Heading to Alaska to be a transport pilot, he had equipped his plane with pontoon landing gear, so he was capable of landing on both land and water, but not mountains. The valley was his safest bet.

The dial in front of him swung as he neared the earth. A glance out his window showed nothing but inky blackness below. It was impossible to know what he was heading into. He felt as if he stood at the altar of his impending wedding once again. The nuptials had never actually occurred, and his bride had returned the ring. Would this be a smooth landing, or another crash and burn?

Kaden lowered the plane as gently as possible, preparing both the dry and wet landing gear of his amphibious aircraft. He strained his vision toward the terrain ahead, and finally his headlamps brought in a reflection that could only be some sort of water. His pontoons would allow him to float, but he still required enough space to slow down. As the water approached, he realized he did not have the space he needed.

Backing up wasn't an option, and he braced himself for the impact after touching down on the black surface. The plane plowed through the water, spraying it up on all sides. He hauled back on the controls, doing his best to slow the aircraft. It fishtailed crazily but continued to barrel toward the shore. He felt as if it happened in slow motion, and yet somehow also too quickly for him to do anything but pray.

The plane met the rocky edge with a deafening crunch, and the abrupt stop launched Kaden forward. His head smacked hard against the controls, and small items sailed through the cabin. Then the aircraft was completely still.

Kaden groaned and reached for his head, his fingers coming away bloody. He fought the urge to close his eyes and give in to unconsciousness. He needed to keep his wits about him. He was in the middle of some of the roughest terrain in the country. It could be days before another human found him. He shut the aircraft's engine down, needing to conserve fuel.

As the propellers slowed to a stop, he pounded the wheel of the plane that was supposed to have been the catalyst of a new life in Alaska. He'd spent every penny of his trust fund to buy it. What would his father say when he learned the plane had made it only one state away? Kaden could easily imagine the smug expression on the man's face.

Kaden took a deep breath to refocus. He couldn't let his divide with his parents make the situation worse. He opened the door to step out and heard howling off in the mountains. It was summer, so the bears were likely out foraging and wolves on the hunt. Kaden might be safer inside the plane until daybreak, but first he had to check his surroundings. Keeping the door wide and the control board's lights illuminated as well as his landing lights, he stood on top of one of the pontoons and inspected the rocky shore.

The illuminated area appeared to be a dense forest. He saw a faint light through the pitch-dark foliage, but it was from a far-off location on the other side of the water. Still, it signified human life. Although he questioned what sort of human would live so remotely. They might not appreciate his intrusion, and the trek toward the light could prove dangerous. Tree roots, canyons, and wild animals could lie anywhere between him and that soft glow. One harrowing episode was enough for the evening. Besides, by the time he circled the lake and made it through the thick tree growth, the sun would be up. He might as well wait until he could see in front of his face.

At least the top of the plane was intact. The craft appeared lodged on a boulder, so the undercarriage could be damaged. He wouldn't know until he moved the plane to dry land, which wouldn't happen that night.

After climbing back inside, he dropped into his seat, deflated but grateful to be alive. It could have been worse. The mountains around him could have claimed him. Kaden steeled himself for the long night ahead. If he couldn't handle the wait, then he had no business hopping around the untamed lands of Alaska. There would be plenty of times when the weather and terrain would ground him, but that suited him fine. At least he would be calling the shots over his own life.

To think he'd nearly given up his freedom for a marriage of "opportunity," as his parents called it. They would never forgive him for their financial loss. He would never forgive them for treating him like a bargaining piece in a business arrangement.

Kaden put on his headset and pressed the radio controls to inform the closest air traffic controller that he was down but safe. He spoke his call name into the microphone, hoping to explain that he had experienced possible hypoxia and been forced to land. Lowering his altitude had proven harrowing with the mountains, but he'd managed to bring the plane down in some sort of valley between the peaks. He wouldn't know more until daylight. Then he would be able to see his actual surroundings. All he could be certain of was that he was in the middle of nowhere.

"Do you read?" he asked when he was met with silence in return.

When no response came, he removed the headset and tossed it over the panel. All he could hope for was that he did have a signal and someone had heard his plea. He searched the cockpit for his phone. It wasn't where he had left it, but any item not strapped down had been tossed around during the rough landing. He felt around and finally located the device under a seat. The screen showed no service.

No radio. No cell. He really was cut off from the world.

"Francesca, where do you think you're going?" Papa rushed out onto the long porch of the 1930s ranch house, waving his arms over his head. His pajama top was unbuttoned and tucked haphazardly into his jeans. Obviously, he had rushed getting dressed to stop her. His cowboy boots slammed against the old wood boards and down the steps.

Halfway into the truck, Frankie Stiles cringed. She'd been caught. "I thought you were asleep. I didn't want to wake you until I was sure, but I think a plane might have crash-landed out back. I won't know until I check it out. Go back to bed. If I find something, I'll come for you." She jumped up in the high seat and cranked the key twice before the old diesel ignition fired. As she reached to close the door, her father caught it.

"Which direction? I'm coming with you." He sought the dark horizon in the correct direction as if he knew the answer already. Had he heard the plane as well?

Frankie had been tending to her restless horse in the barn when she'd heard an engine and a horrible crunching sound echo off the mountains. She'd sprinted into the house to grab the keys, not expecting her father to follow her out.

Frankie rolled her eyes. "Papa, I'm twenty-five years old. At some point, you're going to have to let me do some things on my own around here." She couldn't hide the frustration in her voice. "If I'm going to run this farm someday, I should know the extent of our land and be able to protect it myself." She glanced toward where she had heard the sounds in the dark of night. "And I can't be afraid of anything out there."

"You don't run Nighthawk Farm yet, and as long as I'm in charge, I will accompany you to the back forty acres," her father argued. "Too much has happened out there to let you go gallivanting alone in the middle of the night. Scoot over. I'm driving."

Frankie grimaced but obeyed. Her father really meant that one big thing had happened out there. But it was really big, and so for that, Frankie clambered over to the passenger seat, relinquishing the wheel.

She peered out into the darkness, to where their land touched the river and abutted a northern mountain range. They lived and worked in a long stretch of a Washington valley, sandwiched between other mountain ranges near the Canadian border. Being so far north, away from populated cities, limited their contact with anyone but a few neighboring farms and ranches. Some specialized in livestock, but Nighthawk Farm grew apples. As they passed by rows of trees in the orchard, she didn't know what she had been thinking in trying to rush out to that portion of the property alone. She avoided the other side of the lake by day. What made her think she could handle its eeriness by night? She began to apologize to her father for her lapse in judgment.

But Frankie's throat went dry at the sight of the revolver sticking out of his waistline on his right side.

"What's that for?" she asked.

Papa didn't answer her question at first. The truck creaked and jolted over rutted land until Frankie thought her teeth would be shaken from her head. The headlights bounced over a dirt path that led to the lake. "Until I know the nature of this event, I'll remain cautious. I won't lose you too."

"It's been twenty-five years since my mother died," she countered in the dim cabin.

Her father frowned, the dashboard lights casting shadows over his weathered farmer's face. "I will never know what lured my Vera out here that day. Why she made such a choice. Maybe she thought she was helping somehow." He grew quiet, stopping short of explaining how or why her mother had drowned in the lake.

Frankie didn't press him to say more. Experience had taught her it wouldn't do any good, and she might never learn the details of her mother's death. Not when Chris Stiles refused to talk about her.

The conversation always ended in the same place. In Frankie's mind, her mother's accidental death would forever remain a mystery.

If it had even been an accident.

Silence filled the truck's cabin as they neared the water. The lake on their property was connected to a river that flowed down from Canada and split into thinner tentacles of water. The appendages spread out through the crevices between the bases of the mountains like gnarled fingers, claiming as much territory as they could. One of those branches fed the deep crater that served as a watering source for the farm. Many neighboring farmers wished they had such a source, but Frankie hated the lake that had claimed her mother when Frankie was still a baby. She avoided the far side of it altogether.

Until now.

"You're sure you saw a plane?" Papa asked. He sat hunched forward, his short, stout body close to the steering wheel as he squinted through the windshield.

Frankie also leaned forward with her fingers gripping the seat's edge. "I didn't see anything. I was in the barn. But I heard something that sounded like a crunch. The sound echoed off the mountains. Maybe whatever it was hit the lake."

On a particularly horrendous bounce, the truck's headlight beams exposed a plane perched on a rocky ledge on the far side of the lake.

"There it is," he said, pointing. "It is a plane."

"Figures it would be on that side of the lake," she grumbled, thinking of the memorial her father had erected there in honor of her mother. "We'll have to take the road around and get as close as possible."

When they'd gone as far as they could in the truck, Papa shut down the engine and checked the revolver for bullets.

"Do you really need to have that out?" Frankie asked.

"For all I know, this pilot is smuggling drugs over the border. I'm here to help, but I'm not foolish enough to step into an unknown situation and offer assistance without a way to defend us if the need arises."

Frankie rolled her eyes, but she did feel safer heading out there with some kind of weapon. Her father was right. The pilot could be bad news. Aside from a few farmhands and Trudy, the nanny who had taken care of Frankie in her youth, not too many people ventured so far from civilization.

Frankie and her father exited at the same time and met at the front of the truck. The headlights remained ablaze, and a figure of a person could be seen slumped in the pilot's seat.

Is he dead?

She pushed the thought away as fast as it had come.

"Hello?" she called out. "Are you all right?" Her voice grew louder, and the person inside sat up straight.

The side door opened, and a man stepped out. Standing on the aircraft's pontoon, he held up a hand to shield his eyes. The headlights were blinding him. "I'm sorry to bother you. My name's Kaden Phillips, and I had to make an emergency landing."

"What's your business out here?" Papa demanded.

Frankie gaped at her father's abrasiveness. "Papa, the man nearly died. Go easy." She turned toward the stranger. "Mr. Phillips, it seems you're stuck on the rocks, so be careful coming down. These rocks are treacherous."

"Isn't that going a little too easy?" Papa huffed.

Frankie gently jabbed her father with an elbow as the pilot made his way carefully down the stony terrain. "Behave. We don't have reason to suspect him of anything yet."

Once on the ground, Kaden looked back at his plane and groaned. "It's worse than I thought. I couldn't tell in the dark, but from this angle and with the headlights, it's clear I have a big project ahead of me. The wing may need to be replaced, which will be nothing short of a miracle out here. And I don't know how I'll get it off that boulder."

"At least you're alive," Frankie said.

"There is that." He faced them, his hand outstretched for a handshake. "I am so thankful you came to my rescue."

Frankie almost gasped at the sight of him in the full light.

Kaden Phillips was a handsome man. He wore his black hair cut short and perfectly neat. He could have stepped off a page in a magazine rather than from a downed plane. Aside from the bloody wound on the top of his head, she would have never known he had narrowly escaped death less than an hour before. The man obviously held his cool under pressure.

He also still held his hand out to her.

Frankie tucked a loose strand of brown hair behind her ear and shook his hand. Their touch was brief, but she clasped her fingers together after to hold their contact. "I'm sorry you've had to go through this, but there's not much we can do out here tonight. If it's all right with my father, you can stay in our barn. It's nothing glamorous, but you'll be safe there. Our neighbor, Greg Mullen, has a satellite phone you can use tomorrow."

Papa grunted in what she took to be assent.

"Thank you so much. That would be great. I don't have any cell reception."

"You won't, out here." She led the way back to the truck. "What happened?" She climbed in and slid to the center of the bench seat. Kaden hopped in beside her as Papa came around the driver's side.

The lights of the dashboard illuminated Kaden's perfect teeth flashing in an awkward grin. "It was the strangest thing. I was blinded by a flash of light. At least I think I was. The next thing I knew I was going down."

"What sort of light? There's nothing out here." Nothing but her mother's memory.

"Where were you headed?" Papa asked, backing out and starting down the bumpy path.

"Alaska, for a fresh start as a pilot."

Papa huffed. "The owner of that plane might have something to say about that."

Frankie elbowed her father again and said to Kaden, "I'm sure he will be grateful that you saved his plane from wrecking it completely. And that you're alive and well."

Kaden's smile evaporated, and he stared out into the darkness. "The plane is mine. And there's no way I can afford to replace it. Fixing it is my only option. As far as anyone caring, I'm on my own. And that suits me. Are the two of you alone out here?"

Frankie started to reply, but her father cut her off. "We'll get you to town in the morning, and you can be on your way."

"Papa. Don't be rude." To Kaden, she said, "He gets cranky when he's tired. You can stay as long as you need to get your plane up and running again. And yes, it's the two of us. Later in the summer, we'll have a few farmhands to help us harvest the orchards. If you're still here in a few weeks, you'll meet them."

"No offense, but I hope I'm not. I have a job in Alaska I need to get to," Kaden said.

"Good," Papa said gruffly.

It was the last sound until they reached the barn. Kaden's presence was obviously unwelcome by her father.

But why? What was it about the man that her father distrusted? He didn't even know Kaden.

Did he?

Frankie shook off the ridiculous idea. As they reached the house, she did her best to show hospitality to the stranger who had literally crashed into their lives. When she mentioned the room in the barn, her father said he would take care of it and instructed her to return to the house. There was nothing welcoming in his voice.

At the door to the kitchen, Frankie glanced back to see Kaden heading into the barn and wondered if he would still be there in the morning.

"*Will* you be joining me at church today?" Papa asked Frankie at the breakfast table. The sun rose over the mountains in the east and cast a golden glow across the red-and-white checkered tablecloth.

Frankie took a sip of her coffee and set the cup back on the saucer with a soft clatter. She took a deep breath before responding to her father. After last night when he'd sent her inside, they hadn't said a word to each other. She wouldn't be surprised if he had told Kaden that he had to be gone by morning.

"That all depends on if Kaden Phillips is still here." She raised her gaze to her father to wait for his response.

"I didn't tell him to leave if that's what you mean. I assume the man is still out there. For now." He approached the table and stood behind a chair with his hands resting on top of the ladder-back.

"Why wouldn't you let me help him last night?" Frankie asked.

"He's a stranger on my property. I wasn't about to let my daughter set him up in the loft. I know nothing about this man and where he came from. And the sooner he's gone, the better."

"So you had my best interests at heart?" Her tone betrayed her skepticism.

"Absolutely. Why would you question that?" Papa's bushy white eyebrows furrowed on his wrinkled forehead. The sincerity in his expression made Frankie reconsider her anger. The man had raised her single-handedly, aside from Trudy, who had helped in Frankie's younger years. He always had her best interests at heart, to say nothing of her safety.

And yet, the stifling feeling continued to grow.

"Forgive me, Papa. We don't get too many visitors out here, and the way you treated Mr. Phillips last night made me wonder if that was why. The man was injured, and you wouldn't even let me get him some ice. We could have been a bit more hospitable to someone in a tough situation."

Her father pulled the chair out and sat, resting his arms on the table on either side of his full plate. "I checked on him this morning, and he is fine. I showed him where he could wash up last night. He doesn't need a nursemaid fussing over him. So I'll ask you again. Will you be joining me for church today?"

Very rarely did Frankie miss church. As her father lifted his fork to dig into his breakfast potatoes, she pondered what would happen if she decided not to attend. The thought of refusing appealed to her, not because she wanted to skip out on church, but more as a way of spreading her wings.

"I think I will remain here in case Mr. Phillips needs assistance." It was a valid reason, she thought. She hoped it held less bite for her father. To say what was really on her mind could hurt his feelings. At some point, he would have to step back from controlling her life. Whenever she broached the subject, he reminded her that everything he had was hers, including the farm. The conversation always ended in the same way, with Frankie setting aside her feelings for the responsibilities Nighthawk Farm required of her. She loved her father and their land, but she hated feeling trapped. Whenever he used the farm against her, that was exactly how she felt.

"I suppose I can send Greg over here so that you're not alone," Papa said, mentioning their closest neighbor.

Frankie stood abruptly and brought her empty plate to the sink, dropping it in a bit harder than necessary. She spun around and crossed her arms in front of her, leaning against the old Formica counter. As far as she knew, her father and mother had bought the house before Frankie was born.

The kitchen was situated in the corner of the single-story ranch. It had an entrance out onto the long porch that extended along the whole side of the house. There were three doors along the porch into each part of the house, with the next room being the living room, and the third, her father's bedroom. Frankie's bedroom was on the other side of the house and did not have its own entrance. When she questioned the reason behind it, Papa's excuse was always that it was for her protection.

"And who's going to protect me against Greg?" she asked with a lift of her chin. "Because we both know Greg's intentions are not pure. He wants our land, and he thinks he can get it if I marry him, which I have no intention of doing."

Her father took a gulp of his coffee. "Right now, I trust him more than I trust that pilot. And speaking of him, perhaps I can drop him off at Greg's ranch. He has to use Greg's satellite phone to call for help anyway."

"Papa, there's no reason to distrust Mr. Phillips. He's done nothing wrong, and he needs our help. Why won't you let me help him?" She stopped short of calling her father paranoid, apt as the description was. It made no sense. "We've had farmhands on the property before and you've never had a problem with them. Why does this bother you so much?"

"I hired those men. They had to pass background checks first."

Frankie didn't doubt that her father was planning to run one on Kaden. If he hadn't started already. She doubted he would let Kaden stay much longer, regardless of the results of such a check.

"You can't protect me forever," she said. "You won't be around forever. And before you get on the subject again, I am not marrying Greg." She left off the fact that the man was nearly twenty years older than she was. She wouldn't be able to depend on him either. "I can handle myself."

Her father stood and came over to her, holding out his hands. "Francesca, you don't understand the darkness of this world. There are people who—"

She cut him off. "Who what? Who are these people you're talking about, and what do they want to do that's so threatening?"

"They want to hurt you. Take you from me. I know you don't understand, but I have seen the world and the evil in it. All I want to do is protect you from it."

Though the anguish in his eyes gave her pause, Frankie pressed ahead, desperate for answers she knew she might never receive. She knew he had always kept something from her—something big. "Papa, you sound paranoid. I go to church and see people. I went to community college and saw people. No one wanted to hurt me. And neither does Mr. Phillips. I'm staying home from church to help him today. It would be a charitable thing to do. Plus, the sooner he gets help, the sooner he can be on his way."

Tears glistened in her father's gray-blue eyes, so much like her own. "Will he take you with him?"

Frankie sputtered. "What? That's absurd. First of all, I would never leave with a stranger. Second, Nighthawk Farm is my home, and I love it here." She gazed out the window by the kitchen door. Rows of flourishing apple trees extended as far as the eye could see. They crested the hill and continued beyond. "I can't believe you're afraid I'll leave this place. When have I ventured anywhere and not returned? I went to school and got an accounting degree so that I could run the orchard business. I want to bring our farm into this century, not leave it behind. Don't worry about me leaving, Papa."

"Promise?" The pleading in her father's eyes once again made her feel that she was being manipulated.

"I promise that I have no intention of ever leaving here. I love this place as much as you do." She glanced out in the direction of the memorial to her mother, as well as the downed plane. "Though I'm surprised you've wanted to stay here yourself. You say you want safety, but Mama wasn't safe here. And neither was Mr. Phillips last night. Both of these situations should tell you that the dangers of the world will fall on this doorstep too. We don't have to leave to find them. Danger can find us right here."

Her father's eyes darkened with stark fear. "Francesca, you had better hope and pray that it never does." With that he left, slamming the door behind him. She heard the truck start up and roar down the gravel path to the dirt road that would lead to the nearest town, forty-five minutes away. Perhaps her father thought he had protected them from danger, but Frankie wasn't so naive.

But she did wonder what danger he was so afraid of.

Kaden shrank into the shadows of the long porch and watched as the truck disappeared down the lane. He had been on his way up to the ranch house from the barn when he overheard father and daughter arguing. He didn't want to intrude, but he heard his name. He wasn't surprised. After all, it wasn't every day a plane landed on someone's property. Still, he stayed put to listen to the conversation from the side of the house. The open doors allowed for airflow but also eavesdropping. Kaden supposed the two had never needed to worry about that before.

Once the truck was out of view, he listened as the daughter loudly washed the dishes and cleaned up the kitchen. It was obvious to him by the sounds that the conversation had left her angry. He made his way carefully along the wooden porch, testing the boards before he put his full weight on them so he wouldn't give himself away. He peeked through the window beside the door and found that her back was to him as she scrubbed the dishes in the sink. Her long brown hair brushed her waistline, where an apron was tied in a neat bow over a pair of blue jeans and a yellow T-shirt. She wore a pair of cowboy boots that had obviously seen their fair share of mud. Her work ethic would probably put his to shame.

She shut off the faucet and grabbed a towel to start drying the dishes.

What was he doing, spying on the woman in her own home? He backed up a few steps, then reapproached the door with his usual amount of volume.

"Mr. Phillips?" she called.

Kaden stepped into her view and entered the kitchen. "Good morning . . . Francesca? Is that your name?"

"Frankie is fine. Papa calls me Francesca, but the farmhands have always called me Frankie, and I like it better." She put the plate on the counter and dried her hands, studiously avoiding eye contact.

Kaden guessed that she felt uncomfortable with him around. "I can wait in the barn for your father to return if you would rather."

"No. You're fine. Please, have a seat. I can fry some eggs and potatoes if you'd like. Would that work for you?"

"You don't have to go to any trouble for me. You've already done so much."

"Sit," she instructed, gesturing to the table. "I won't hear another word about it. You are our guest."

Kaden lifted his hands in surrender and took his seat. "Now that you mention it, I am quite hungry." He smiled at his pretty hostess. "I haven't eaten since I left Boise last night."

Frankie moved about the kitchen as if she'd been doing it her whole life, which she likely had. Kaden wondered where her mother might be, if she still had one. He decided not to ask because he didn't want to pry, but he couldn't imagine his own mother sailing around a kitchen to whip up breakfast for him. He'd grown up with maids and cooks, but that life was in the past.

"Boise? Is that where you're from?" Frankie cracked the eggs into a sizzling pan.

"In a little town right outside the city. My family works in software. Have you been there?"

Frankie shook her head, causing her silky hair to swing against her back. "I haven't been much farther than a couple of hours from here. I attended a community college for two years, but I commuted. What's it like?"

Kaden shrugged, trying to imagine what it might be like to remain in one place his whole life, especially a place so different from the cities he was used to. The idea made him question his hosts, and he secretly vowed to make tracks fast. Something felt off in the place, no matter how nice it felt to have a pretty young woman make him breakfast.

"I grew up in a city with mountains to the north, so we had mild winters."

She flipped his eggs with the spatula, then scooped fried potatoes on his plate. "I've never been to a city. Are there tall buildings?"

Kaden found himself pitying Frankie. He also realized how much he took for granted, having grown up thinking his life was like everyone else's.

"How old are you?" he asked.

She switched off the burner, then tipped the frying pan and let the two eggs slip onto a plate. She headed in his direction, her steps soft against the faded and cracked linoleum. "I hope you like it. I'm twenty-five, and you?"

"Twenty-eight. I thought you were way younger than me, but we're close in age." Perhaps it was her innocence that had led to that thought. "And yes, there are tall buildings. Lots of them. Perhaps someday you'll get to travel more."

She shook her head and sat beside him. "Papa is getting older, and I pretty much run the farm now. I don't see myself ever moving away, but that's okay. I love it here." She glanced out the window beyond his shoulder. "You said you were on your way to Alaska for a job?"

"Yes, I plan to charter my new plane as a commuter pilot." Kaden frowned, thinking about his broken aircraft on the other side of the property. "I really need to fix it quickly. My new life is waiting for me, and the longer it takes for me to get there, the more it confirms that my parents were right about me."

She tilted her head, swinging her hair against the table. "What did they say about you?"

"I let them down by not following through with the plan they had for me. I was supposed to marry an heiress to a huge fortune, but when I told her I wanted to relocate to Alaska, she changed her mind. The fact that I wasn't upset about it tells me it never would have worked. But it meant my parents lost both financial and social advantages that they'd been counting on. They would like nothing better than for me to return to Idaho with my tail between my legs. So you see, I need to fix my plane and get to Alaska before they find out there was a problem. At this point, there could already be a search team looking for my downed plane because I didn't arrive last night as scheduled."

She folded her hands on the table and studied him. "What was it like to tell them you were leaving?"

Kaden had a feeling that Frankie was asking him for personal reasons. He had no desire to cause conflict between her and her father. He barely escaped a conflict of his own with his parents, and that was enough for him.

On the other hand, he refused to lie to her. "I suppose it was scary. No one wants to disappoint their family. But when I finally made the decision, I knew it was right for me." He couldn't help but wonder if she had ever wanted to tell her father that she was leaving. Instead, he changed the subject. "As soon as I can contact an airport with a hangar, I'll see about fixing the wing there, and I'll be out of your hair."

"You're not going anywhere."

The cryptic words gave him pause. He wasn't even sure where he was on a map, and if he had landed in an unsafe place, would he ever even be found?

"Excuse me?" His voice sounded thick to his ears.

"It's Sunday. Nothing's open. The closest town is forty-five minutes away, and my dad took the truck. We don't have Internet or phone service. But our neighbor, Greg, has a satellite phone and Internet. I could take you over there later today so you can contact someone. How does that sound?"

Kaden relaxed a little. Her explanation sounded much less threatening than he'd feared.

"I think first I'd like to head out to the plane and assess the damage. If it's not too bad, I might be able to repair it enough here to be on my way." He hoped that would be the case. He didn't feel safe on the strange farm in the middle of nowhere. As sweet as Frankie presented herself, he didn't know her at all. And it was clear that the sooner he made himself scarce, the happier her father would be. He intended to make that happen as quickly as possible.

3

$\mathcal{F}$rankie had saddled up two horses for the ride out to the crash site, and then Kaden had to make some calls. For him, she would make an exception and take him to Greg's house to use the satellite phone.

If only Papa would embrace the current century, she thought. She would give anything for the modern conveniences that would make their lives easier.

"How are you handling the horse?" Frankie asked Kaden as he rode a Clydesdale named Blossom alongside her.

"He's bigger than I'm used to, but I'm staying on."

Kaden had assured her that he could ride, having spent many years playing polo at his family's country club. Some of the things he said were so foreign to her. She wasn't even sure what a country club was.

"Is your country club in the country?" she asked as their horses' hooves raised clouds of dust from the dirt path lined with apple trees.

Kaden offered her a kind smile, but it made her feel as if she'd said something wrong. He reached up and grabbed an apple from a nearby tree. He took a huge bite, then grimaced and spat it out as politely as possible in the tall grass along the path.

"Those aren't ready for picking," she said, barely holding back a laugh.

"That should answer your question about my country club." He swiped at his lips to remove the flavor of the unripe fruit. "This is more country than I have seen in my whole life, and it appears I have a few things to learn."

"Especially if you're going to live in Alaska. Are you sure you're ready for that?"

"More than ready. Besides, I'll be flying over the wild countryside, but living in the city."

"Hopefully, you don't have to make any more emergency landings." Frankie glanced off in the direction of where his plane had come to a stop. She couldn't believe she was going out to the back forty acres twice in as many days. "I have a confession to make."

Kaden waited politely for her to continue. The man was especially handsome. His black hair glistened in the sunlight, and his bright blue eyes were full of compassion. She thought it strange of him to watch her in that way, yet comforting at the same time.

"I don't know why I'm telling you this, but my mother died in the lake that you landed on last night."

His horse came to a stop, and she followed his lead. "I'm sorry to hear that. Did she drown?"

"I don't really know. It happened when I was a baby, right after we moved here and bought the farm. My father doesn't talk too much about it, but there's a memorial out there. She's from the city like you. Papa says she couldn't handle the hard work of the farm. There are many hazards in farm life. Perhaps she was too weak to handle a horse and was thrown. All Papa told me was that he found her body in the water."

"What was her name?"

"Vera Stiles."

"Which would make your name Frankie Stiles. I like it." His smile had returned, and it put her at ease. "Thank you for sharing about your mom. Something tells me you don't do that often."

She used her knees to get the horse moving again. "Never, actually. It was easier than I thought it would be. I don't remember anything about her. I have one photo of her. It was taken before we moved here, right after I was born. Papa says I could be her twin."

"Then she must have been beautiful."

Kaden's horse kept in step with hers, so Frankie had to duck her head to shield her blush at his words. No one had ever been so forward with her. The farmhands never would have dared, and Trudy had been stingy with her compliments. Not even Greg had ever said that to her, and he ostensibly wanted to marry her.

Her horse stumbled over something along the trail, saving her from having to respond. "Whoa." She pulled back on the reins to right Shadow, her Tobiano American Paint. Patting the side of the animal's black-and-white flank, Frankie said, "That was my fault. I should have been watching the trail. Good girl."

As they approached the lake, the sprawling mountain ranges grew higher with sharper peaks. Stones and boulders dotted the landscape as they left the orchards behind. Old avalanche paths cut the terrain along the sides of the mountains, signs of the harsh climate during winter. Wind whistled through rustling trees, and Frankie lifted her face to the breeze.

"You don't have to come out here with me." Kaden cut into her thoughts. "I mean, if it's too hard for you. I could be out here for a while."

She set her chin stubbornly. "This is my property. I should have no problem traveling over any part of it. It's not so much that I fear the land itself, but rather my mother's death." Frankie faced forward again.

"Drowning would be terrifying. I understand why the idea makes you uncomfortable."

"I wasn't talking about drowning."

"No? Then what?"

Was she giving too much away to a stranger? "My father can be overprotective."

"No way. I don't believe it." He barely hid his smile.

"I'm being serious. I know he means well, but there are times when his behavior is stifling. As I get older, I wonder if my mother felt the same way. If she felt smothered enough, would she have done something reckless to escape?"

"I see." Kaden took a deep breath, then said, "I overheard you and your father talking this morning. I didn't mean to eavesdrop, but your voices carried out to the barn. As I got closer, I could tell there was a problem. Is he keeping you here against your will?"

Frankie considered the question, which seemed to have arisen out of genuine concern. "I wouldn't go that far. I'm free to go if I want to. But I don't."

Kaden released the reins with one hand and held it up to her. "Hey, I'm not judging you at all. My parents pretty much arranged my marriage to that heiress I was telling you about. Julia called it off when she found out I wanted to go to Alaska." His expression betrayed no resentment.

"You like her," Frankie said. "I don't see any anger toward her on your face."

"I do, but not in that way. We grew up together, and I think we were both doing our parents a favor by agreeing to the arrangement. Alaska may have been her excuse, but I don't believe that she wanted to go through with it any more than I did. How about you? Any boyfriends or proposals?"

"One, I guess. Proposal, not boyfriend."

"A proposal without a boyfriend? That's not usually how things happen anymore. Care to explain?"

Frankie gestured eastward. "Greg Mullen, the man who owns the satellite phone, lives on the ranch adjacent to our property. He would really like to have access to our water rights."

"Ah, a marriage of convenience for him. But what would be in it for you?"

"I don't think marriage should be a business proposition. I think people should marry for love."

The humor left his eyes and was replaced with a bit of sadness. "Frankie Stiles, you could give my family a lesson on that topic."

Frankie was like no one Kaden had ever met. The way she sat on a horse and traversed over the rocky terrain, he could tell she felt at home on the untamed land. He could also tell she was strong both physically and mentally. He found her serene countenance becoming and refreshing. In a world filled with prideful people, he doubted there was an arrogant bone in her body. When he had first met her, he'd thought her naive and easily manipulated, but the more he talked with her, the more he realized he had confused innocence with weakness, and he had been wrong.

As they reached the boundaries of her land, the sound of a squealing engine split the air.

"That's Greg," Frankie said, stopping her horse to wait for a man who approached on an ATV. "Whoa," she consoled the nervous animal over the vehicle's high-pitched engine, which grew louder as it neared.

Kaden's horse danced and huffed, but he pulled the reins back and held the animal still. Did Greg not care for Frankie's safety? Kaden would have to go with the man to use his satellite phone and Internet, but he didn't feel right about it.

"I want to see the plane first," he told Frankie before Greg reached them.

"Are you sure?"

"Maybe I can get it going quickly and be on my way so I won't need his phone."

"Don't you want to call your family?"

"I do, but I don't want to impose." He watched Greg, aghast at the man's audacity in proposing to Frankie. The neighbor had to be at least twenty years older than her.

Greg came to a stop. "Hello, Francesca. Who's your friend?" he asked, without looking Kaden's way.

Irritation threaded the man's voice, and Kaden hid his satisfaction at being the cause.

"This is Kaden. His plane went down on the back forty last night. We're on our way out to the site to assess the damage. Would it be possible for us to stop by later and use your phone? He has to let people know he's safe."

Greg sent a sharp gaze toward him. "Sure, anything for you, Francesca."

The answer didn't feel welcome, and Kaden found himself disappointed by the men in Frankie's life. So far no one seemed to have her best interests in mind. He thought his own family was controlling, but Frankie's situation felt almost dangerous.

"I'm surprised you're going out there, Francesca," Greg continued. "You never make that trek. Are you sure you're up for it? I don't think it's a good idea. I could take your guest out there."

Kaden huffed at Greg's choice of words. Taking someone out wasn't always a good thing. He also didn't like being spoken about as though he weren't there. But besides all that, why would Greg think Frankie shouldn't go out to a site on her own property? Was it because her mother had died there—or was there another reason?

Kaden interjected into the conversation that was about him but didn't include him. "I'll be sure to be on my best behavior. I didn't purposely crash my plane so I could accost a woman. Frankie is safe with me."

"Greg, I'll be fine," Frankie added. "Thank you for your concern, but there's nothing to worry about."

Greg shot an irritated glare toward Kaden, then softened it when he faced Frankie once more. "You know where to find me if you need help. I'm always here for you, you know. What happened to your mom haunts us all."

Kaden realized the man was old enough to have known Vera Stiles. "Do you always ride out here on the Stiles property?" he asked nonchalantly, but the meaning of his words spoke volumes. What business did the man have back there?

Greg revved his engine and let it rumble low. "Sometimes I have a cow that's gone astray. Sometimes I want to be neighborly and pay the Stileses a visit. Nothing wrong with that, right, Francesca?"

Frankie offered a tight smile. It didn't appear she had a say in the matter. Once again, Kaden puzzled over the goings-on out here in the middle of nowhere. Not that it was any of his business. He had one thing to worry about, and it didn't include the Stiles farm. But if Kaden was reading Frankie right, she didn't care for Greg Mullen riding his ATV on her property either.

"See?" Greg said. "We're all happy neighbors watching out for each other. Don't forget that, Mr. Phillips. In that neighborly spirit, my phone is yours to use anytime, of course." With that, Greg gunned the vehicle forward and spun around, spraying dirt toward them from beneath the wheel. He sped off.

The horses pranced again at the sound. Once they were pacified, Kaden said, "He drove off in a different direction. He wasn't coming from his ranch."

"No. He was coming from the crash site. He's probably up to something."

Her response showed Kaden that Frankie was a smart woman. She may have been silenced by the people in her life, but she was quick and wise. Coming from his own family situation, he understood why she put herself last. She wanted to do what was expected of her to keep the peace, even if that meant she never got a chance to live the life she wanted.

Kaden swallowed the words he wanted to say about all he was seeing. It was none of his business. He kicked his horse up to a gallop, not slowing until the lake came into view around a jagged hill. The flourishing land around the water was breathtaking. Lush mountains sprang up from the edges of the water. "The fact that I didn't crash into any of those is a miracle."

She stopped beside him. "That's for sure. It is a beautiful place. Perhaps my mother was drawn to its beauty, and an accident really did happen."

Kaden weighed the words hanging on his tongue. "I don't want to cross a line here, but you say Greg wants your land. Are you sure that's all he wants? Who knows what's in these mountains?"

Frankie mulled over the possibilities he'd painted for her. Finally, she replied, "It doesn't matter what he wants. I'll never marry him."

"I'm glad to hear that, but honestly, he acts like he knows something you don't. He also mentioned your mother. I assume he lived here when she died?"

Frankie nodded.

"And he's very comfortable riding around your property. Like he's done it forever."

She gestured toward the ground. "His tire tracks are everywhere."

"Exactly. You may say you'll never marry him, and he won't get your land, but Frankie, he is already using your land. It's a matter of time before he claims rights to it, and because your father has never stopped him, he might be able to get it. Trust me—my parents made me get a law degree."

"I thought you were a pilot."

He tossed a grin at her. "I got my pilot's license without their knowledge."

She frowned, staring beyond his shoulder. When he followed her gaze, he saw the wrecked plane and nearly crumpled himself. Alaska had been so close, but there he was in the middle of nowhere with a busted aircraft. No working plane meant no job. No job meant his family would expect him home—if they found out where he was.

The thought was unfathomable, but after meeting Greg, Kaden didn't feel so bad not using the man's satellite phone yet. It seemed to come with strings, and Kaden had had enough of strings.

Strings did more than control. They choked the life out of a person.

And he had barely started to breathe.

"*H*ow much damage are you looking at? And you're late," Papa said as Frankie and Kaden sat down at the dinner table.

It didn't feel to Frankie that he was asking out of concern or compassion, but more to start the countdown to Kaden's departure.

"Sorry I was late for dinner, Papa. Thank you for cooking tonight. Time got away from us out at the plane."

"Sir, the plane started right up, so there's nothing wrong with the engine. It's the wing that needs repair," Kaden explained.

"Papa, we would like to move it into the barn so Kaden can work on it tomorrow," Frankie added. "It would be faster and more efficient to fix it here than making the ride out to the lake each day. Would that be all right with you?"

"None of this is all right with me, but if it will speed things along, I'll allow it. I don't know how you'll find parts, though. And I'm not giving you weeks to do so," Papa told Kaden.

"I understand, sir," Kaden said. All mirth was gone from his face. "I may not need parts. In fact, I think I can fix the dent without removing the wing. I may not even need to rewrap it. I spent a lot of time with the team building the plane. I think I can handle the repairs myself. Of course, that's if I can get it off the rocks. Whatever hit my wing couldn't have been very big. Perhaps a large bird. But I'm still not sure where the light came from."

Papa didn't respond. Frankie wasn't sure he was even listening.

Kaden had yet to touch the pan-fried steak Papa had made. Frankie would have cooked, but they had lost track of time at the site. In the daylight, Kaden had been able to assess the damage and was excited to realize that he could manage the repairs. Papa shouldn't have been angry at them for being late.

Kaden picked up his fork and said to Papa, "Thank you for letting me work in the barn. If I can ask for one more thing—do you happen to have a welder I could use?"

Papa chewed slowly before he said, "You'll find it in the barn. Use what you want out there. The tools came with the farm, so they're old, but they work."

"I'm sure it will be fine, thank you. Once I move the plane, I hope to figure out what hit me last night."

"How about you focus on getting out of here and not on playing investigator? The faster you leave, the less chance we'll have the FAA out here. Things won't go well for you if that happens."

Frankie dropped her fork, and it clattered to her plate. She'd had enough of her father's rudeness for one day. "What would make you say such a thing? Kaden could have died out there."

Her father shoved back his chair with a scrape along the linoleum. "You're right. That would have been worse. A body would be harder to hide than a plane. I'll go see about that welder."

Frankie sat in stunned silence until after Papa had left the house and was far enough away not to hear them. Her last bite of food lodged in her throat. She reached for her water glass and took a couple of sips.

"I've never heard him speak to someone like that," she whispered apologetically. "I don't know what has gotten into him."

Kaden's face was ashen, probably mirroring her own. "I feel like I've been dropped off in the twilight zone. Frankie, are you sure I'm safe here? Are *you* safe here?"

"He doesn't trust people. We've had to protect our land from trespassers who wanted the water access."

"I've said nothing about taking your land. I've talked about Alaska constantly. What have I said to make him mention hiding my body?"

"Nothing. It makes no sense for him to distrust you so much. And his being so threatening is uncalled for. I'm sorry. The best thing is to fix your plane as fast as you can so you can go."

Frankie went to the living room and opened the top drawer of her desk. She removed her latest ledger, brought it back to the table, and placed it on the surface between them. "These include all our assets in equipment, which you're welcome to use. I hope it's enough to fix your plane."

Kaden glanced toward the field, where Papa drove Blossom pulling a cart toward the orchard. "Everything is so old-school here." He flipped open the ledger to reveal her neat penmanship. "Even your books are handwritten. Do you not own a computer?"

"I had to use one at the library in college, but Papa forbade it here. He wanted me to stick to our regular ways of keeping the accounts."

"'Forbade' would be the right word. And it's not normal. No offense, but it seems like your father is used to hiding things. A computer could be hacked. A telephone could be tapped. By keeping this farm in the dark ages, he keeps the whole place hidden. I'm surprised he let you go to college."

"I had to fight for it. He approved the community college under the condition that I still lived at home. It was a two-hour drive each way, but worth it. I told him I would be running the farm someday without him, so I needed to stay up on current trends."

Kaden scoffed. "He couldn't have cared too much about staying current."

A laugh escaped her lips before she could stop it. But no other response was needed to his statement. She couldn't deny the truth, and the truth was that Papa had to be hiding something. She had always known it.

But what?

"I suppose I've always wondered if he was running from something or someone," she mused, even as she felt guilty for voicing such personal thoughts against her father.

Kaden covered her hand on the open ledger. He captured her gaze with his striking blue eyes and held it in heavy silence. The jovial moment they had shared vanished in the old kitchen.

"Has he ever hurt you?" Kaden asked seriously.

"Never. Honest." Frankie couldn't look away. If she did, he would think she was lying, and she wasn't. "He's probably acting this way because it's always been the two of us, and maybe he's worried you could change that."

"Not that I plan to do that, but what happens when someone does? He can't expect you to never marry or fall in love? What happens when that comes to pass?"

She bit her lip and turned her attention to a window overlooking the rows of apple trees. The land would be hers someday. Papa was sixty-five years old and still had his strength, but for how long? "There was someone in college I really liked."

"What happened?" Kaden's question sounded far away and muffled by her thoughts.

Her mind snapped back to the present. "It would have never worked." She cleared her throat and changed the subject back to the ledger between them. "Do you think you'll have everything you need here?"

"I think so. With your help here, it could be done in a day, and then I can fly over those mountains and be back on track for Alaska."

Frankie tried to mirror his excitement at the idea, but her smile felt forced. She couldn't fathom why the idea of Kaden leaving in the next day or so made her feel as though she was being left behind. It was ludicrous when Nighthawk Farm was her home, and she loved it. Perhaps the feeling stemmed from Papa's remarks about hiding bodies, which had her on edge. Perhaps she liked Kaden's company and easy smiles and was beginning to imagine what else she was missing out there in the world.

"Have you ever dreamed of what might be beyond your mountains?" Kaden asked, as if he'd read her mind. He'd caught her staring at the glowing peaks as the sun went down behind them.

Frankie pressed her lips tight, not wanting to admit to such a thing. "I love my home."

"I know, but there's nothing wrong with thinking about it. Have you? You can tell me. I won't tell your father."

Her hands were trembling. She clasped them together to hide it.

He covered her hands and brought her chin up. "You don't have to hide anything from me. You can trust me, Frankie. I want to be sure that when I leave here, you'll be safe."

"I will be. Papa would never hurt me." She swallowed hard and nodded. "But yes, I have imagined what's beyond the mountains. Until last night, I never even ventured to the lake. Now . . ."

He didn't respond.

She pushed through the guilt and continued, "Now I think about how much farther I could go. Just to see what's out there. That's all," she finished quickly.

He seemed to bite back a smile and said, "You remind me of a kid caught with her hand in a cookie jar. You have nothing to be ashamed of, and I hope someday you find out what's out there. But not until you're ready, and on your own terms. Trust me when I say it will be amazing.

It's taken me a long time to get here myself, so I would never tell you what to do and when. For me, though, the sky's the limit now. Literally, if I can get there."

"I'm happy for you." Her smile came easily, knowing she meant it. "Maybe someday I'll be able to go check it out. Maybe even come see you as far off as Alaska."

"I would like that, Frankie."

Her heartbeat pulsed in her head at the sweet smile he wore specially for her. She allowed herself to mull over his words about falling in love. It was a topic she never dared to broach. But the ease and comfort she felt with Kaden made her imagine all kinds of possibilities.

"I want you to have the life you want, Frankie. If that's staying on the farm, then I will be happy for you. But if there might be more for you out there, I really hope you find that. It doesn't have to be something as big as my plane. It could be something as simple as someone to share your farm with." He covered her hand with his large warm one.

She stared at his hand on top of hers and finally managed to murmur, "I will consider it."

He beamed at her. "Good," he said, releasing her and picking up the ledger. "Do you mind if I read through your inventory for a bit?"

"Of course." She touched her hand where the heat from his remained.

Kaden dug into his potatoes as he read through her bookkeeping. "You are so thorough and orderly. I may have gone to law school rather than study business, but I can tell you have a skill."

Francesca moved food around on her plate, but dinner was no longer appetizing. "Papa taught me everything I know. I went to college, but experience on the farm outweighed any formal education I had there."

"My parents would hire you in a heartbeat to keep their books, though I would never recommend you work for them. If you ever think you want to branch out from the farm, I'm sure you would find accounting work. You could be really successful out in the world."

"I guess bookkeeping comes naturally for me, which is fortunate since it's also a necessity to running the business."

Kaden lifted his face to her, but it felt as if he were gazing through rather than at her. A strange, stunned expression clouded his blue eyes, then he said, "I can't believe I said any of that. I sounded like my father. Forget everything I just said, Frankie."

"Everything?"

"Well, not the part about your skills. But you do what you want with them. *You* decide, okay?"

"Okay. I guess we both have parents who want the best for us, in their own flawed ways."

"I suppose so, but my dad never threatened to hide any bodies."

His grin had returned, but Frankie found it difficult to laugh at his joke.

Death was never something to laugh about.

$\mathcal{T}$he memorial to Vera Stiles stood under a tree, consisting of a white cross with the words Until Death Do Us Part carved into it. As Kaden approached it around sunrise the next morning, he wondered if Frankie's mother was also buried there at the lake. Frankie hadn't said so, but after Chris's cryptic words the night before about hiding bodies, he found the idea plausible. The carved words on the cross were every bit as puzzling. Rest in Peace would be more appropriate. The message that was there felt like a threat. They were the words of a vow at the beginning of a marriage, not the end. Unless they were meant as a final statement that the marriage was over because Vera's life was over.

A shiver raced up Kaden's spine, and he turned away from the memorial and toward his plane. On his second day at Nighthawk Farm, Kaden hoped to be gone by sunset. It wasn't realistic that he would be able to repair the wing by nightfall, but he would try his hardest.

Bypassing the gnarled tree where he'd tethered Blossom, he approached the glistening lake that seemed so peaceful juxtaposed with his damaged plane. The rocky shoreline was the sole representation of conflict he could see. He needed to maneuver his plane out from the rock's grip. The best way he could see to do so would be to back it into the water and find a clearing with no boulders where he could bring it onto dry land. He hadn't wanted to wake Frankie so early, but he could certainly have used her help.

He touched the dent on the aluminum wing of his plane where the object had hit him in the sky. From what he could tell, there were no punctures in the wing, and Kaden figured he could repair the dent with a technique called glue pulling. He probably wouldn't even have to drill to get inside or have to remove the whole wing to wrap a new skin over it. When he reached Alaska, he could have it resprayed. Frankie's ledger showed he would have everything he needed to repair the aircraft. Kaden felt hopeful for a quick departure—perhaps even that evening—and couldn't wait to tell Frankie.

Frankie.

Kaden's joy diminished at the thought of leaving her behind. It made no sense. Three days ago, he hadn't known she existed. The farm was her home, and she loved it. She'd said so repeatedly. But was that because the isolated place was all she ever knew, all she had ever been allowed to know?

I could show her what's out there, beyond those mountains.

The fanciful thought came to him, but he dismissed it instantly. Frankie wasn't interested in seeing the world. That was his dream. Frankie had no desire to leave her home. He was the one who had wanted to leave his, and he shouldn't project those feelings onto her. Frankie rode horses through her farmland. He flew planes through the wide-open skies. She had her feet planted on the ground. He had his head in the clouds.

"Get it together, Phillips. And get out of here as fast as you can, before you really lose it." He spoke aloud as he climbed into the cockpit and started the plane's engine. The propellers on the nose jumped to life, and Kaden's hope was restored with every revolution. He wouldn't dare fly with the dented wing, but once he got the plane on flat land, he would be one step closer to airborne. The hardest part would be backing the plane out from where the right pontoon was lodged within the rocky shoreline.

Typically, planes didn't go in reverse, but his prop plane could be maneuvered. Kaden sat at the controls and contemplated his best course of action to reverse the plane back into the water and off the rocks. He could move the prop lever to control the propellers, or he could push the throttle all the way aft. Both could produce reverse thrust and move the plane backward. Kaden opted for the throttle first, then the prop lever.

Neither worked. The plane didn't move an inch.

He climbed back out and walked around the spinning blades to push on the wedged pontoon. Leaning into it with all his strength budged it slightly, but he would need more power to get the plane to move any further. He glanced to where Blossom grazed beside her tree but immediately dismissed that option. He didn't have a way to hook her up to the pontoon, and he had no way of knowing how deep the lake was. He wouldn't endanger the horse simply to get his plane free.

"I was so close to escaping this strange place," he muttered as he shoved at the pontoon with all his might, breaking a sweat from the exertion. With each push, Kaden saw his hopes of getting out of Nighthawk Farm by nightfall fade away.

As Frankie rode her horse toward the lake, she heard an ATV roaring up behind her. She knew without checking that it was Greg. Who else would be out there on a four-wheeler when her father didn't bother with modern equipment?

"Whoa." She slowed Shadow to a halt. When Greg pulled up beside them, she asked him, "What brings you out onto my land again so soon?"

"I should ask you the same thing. I can count on one hand the number of times you've made this trek in your whole life, and two of those were yesterday and today."

"The fact that you know this makes me question your reason for being here even more. Does Papa know you cross the border onto our land so often?"

"Your father and I have an agreement. You don't need to worry your pretty head about it."

Frankie bit her tongue to stop herself from letting the man know how condescending he sounded. "Nighthawk Farm will be mine someday. Don't forget that. Any verbal deals you negotiated with Papa won't carry over."

Greg's smile irked her. "You think so? Francesca, I know things about your father. Things you would never want anyone else to find out. Trust me."

Frankie felt as if her world had tipped on its axis the night Kaden landed on her farm. She had woken that morning hoping it had been a nightmare. She hated thinking her father had done something as sinister as his words about hiding bodies had implied. Greg behaving in a know-it-all fashion was too much when Frankie knew next to nothing about her father's past.

"What did my father do?" she demanded.

He smirked. "Information comes at a price. And you know what that price is."

Frankie knew what he wanted. It was what he had always wanted.

"The answer will always be no," she said. "Get that through your head. I will not marry you or anyone else who is only interested in getting their hands on my land."

"And how do you know this pilot is any different?"

Frankie scoffed. "Kaden wants to get out of here as quickly as possible. I have no reason to worry about him attempting to take what belongs to me."

Greg chuckled and shook his head. Even though she sat high above him, he made her feel so small.

"You have no idea what a gold mine this land is, Frankie. Such a shame." He shut off the engine, and as soon as he did, they could hear the airplane off in the distance.

Frankie gently kicked her heels and the horse raced forward. "He's got the plane running!"

Greg restarted the ATV and drove alongside her to the lake. Across the water, Frankie saw Kaden struggling to push the pontoon away from the rock. The back half of the plane still sat in the water, and she could see it inching with each push.

She picked up speed and rode her horse over to help, but she slowed when she saw Greg pass her on his four-wheeler. Kaden's stunned face must have matched her own when her neighbor drove his ATV up to the pontoon. "Let's see if I can help with this," Greg said.

Kaden climbed into the cockpit to work the controls, and after a few seconds of the ATV squealing, the plane dislodged from the shore and floated backward onto the water. He jumped out onto a pontoon, waving his arms in triumph. The joy on his face spoke volumes.

Kaden was one step closer to leaving.

Frankie wanted to be happy for him, and she began to question why a moment that should have been something to celebrate felt to her like something to mourn. Nothing made sense anymore. Three days ago, she hadn't even known the man. His presence had upended everything and made her take stock of her entire life, especially Papa's history. Even Greg knew things about her father that she didn't.

What had Papa done?

Kaden jumped to shore, a huge grin on his handsome face. He approached Greg with his hand extended to shake. "Thank you, man. That was exactly what I needed."

Frankie watched the exchange between them and thought how the day before, Kaden hadn't trusted Greg. But the man had helped him, so everything seemed to have changed.

She stood back and observed how the tables had turned so fast. She felt like an outsider as Kaden and Greg bonded over their success. She ducked her head, not wanting Kaden to see that she wasn't as excited as she ought to have been. Her mind whirled with what Greg had insinuated to her about her father. She didn't trust Greg, but she also hesitated to interrupt their celebration.

As she walked over to where the plane had come ashore, she noticed something black wedged between the rocks.

Picking it up, she noticed that it was made of plastic, and there were more pieces in the rocks. Kaden's plane was white, but where else would the piece have come from? "Are these broken pieces from your plane?"

"What?" Kaden approached her and took the object from her hand. "I have no idea what this is. I don't think it came from my plane."

Suddenly, Greg was beside her, gathering the largest piece that was still intact. He held it up for them to see.

"It's a drone," Kaden said in surprise. "Or it was before it hit my aircraft. I must have dragged it all the way down. That explains the flash of light right before impact. Is the camera still on it?"

The two men bent to appraise the mangled piece of equipment, but Frankie didn't miss how Greg had yet to release it. He kept it close as Kaden searched beneath it.

"It's still there. Maybe we can figure out a way to watch the recorded footage on it. We might be able to see the owner on the recording."

Kaden sifted through the other pieces scattered among the rocks. "If we find a serial number, the FAA can identify who it belongs to as well. Everyone has to register their drones."

Greg flipped over the piece he held to examine the camera. "I can take this back to my house and try to view the footage on my computer."

"That would be great," Kaden said.

"No," Frankie said at the same time.

Both men raised their eyebrows in question at her abrupt refusal of Greg's offer. But she didn't trust Greg's intentions as much as Kaden seemed to. For all she knew, Greg had been out on her property the last two days because he was trying to locate his drone, the one in his hands that he'd yet to relinquish.

"Frankie, I'm the one with the setup at home to view any recordings. Your dad refuses to modernize at all, remember?"

Greg's point felt like a dig. Once again, the man acted as though he had the upper hand.

Because he did.

Annoyance flared within her again at Papa's attempts to keep the outside world away from the farm. Kaden's presence proved that danger would find them regardless of her father's attempts to shield them. Kaden could be taken advantage of by Greg, and he didn't even realize it. Frankie reasoned that if the drone belonged to Greg, he probably hadn't meant to hit Kaden's plane with it. The man was probably using it over her property at night for something more personal—perhaps he was searching for something.

"Is the drone yours?" she asked Greg pointedly. She watched for any sign of guilt but saw none. Maybe he was hiding it well.

Kaden leaned back, appearing to understand her concern. He held out his hand for the drone. "Why don't I hold onto it for now?"

Greg scoffed. "This is unreal. I can't believe you think this is mine.

But fine, take it. I was trying to help." He passed the mangled metal and plastic to Kaden. "You can still bring it over to view the footage. I understand you need to protect yourself, but we don't know each other, so I have no reason to wish you harm."

Kaden peered at Frankie, seeking silent input on Greg's offer.

"I guess we don't really have a choice," she said. To Greg, she warned, "I'll be watching your every move. And don't assume that because I don't own a computer, I don't understand them. I know more than you think."

Greg snorted. "How?"

"You've been counting down the days until I take over the farm, and so have I. Whether Papa likes it or not, I'll be bringing Nighthawk Farm into the future. And no—you will not be a part of it."

$\mathcal{G}$reg Mullen's sprawling horse ranch was a beautiful property that included a large white barn and a two-story log cabin. If not for the dying grass, Kaden would have thought the ranch was thriving. But the wide-open pastures with the tracks from Greg's ATV showed signs of drought, and Kaden had to ponder what a man would do if faced with such challenges.

Perhaps scope out ways to reroute the neighbor's water source to his property, and a drone could come in handy to accomplish that plan.

"Any sign of a serial number?" Frankie asked as Greg entered his house. A large German Shepherd growled at the sight of them at the door.

"Leo, be nice," Greg told the dog. "Don't mind him. He doesn't see too many strangers out here."

Frankie held out her hand for the dog to sniff while Kaden showed her the place where a number might have been on the drone's tail, but had been scratched off.

"Do you think the tail number was scratched off during the accident—or beforehand, on purpose?" she asked.

"To be out late at night on your property tells me that whoever navigated the drone wanted to remain anonymous." Kaden eyed Greg as the man sat down at a computer desk and booted up his PC.

If the drone was his, Greg was running full speed ahead to show them. The man acted as if he had nothing to hide. So maybe he didn't. At least not about the drone. The man was up to something, but Kaden didn't think he'd caused the plane crash.

Frankie was another story. The way she watched Greg with such scrutiny suggested she had many reasons not to trust the man. Kaden had to believe her reasons were valid. She had a lifetime of experiences living near Greg, while Kaden had two days on which to judge his character.

"I'm ready," Greg told them. "Pass it over and I'll try to connect the camera to download the footage."

Kaden glanced Frankie's way, and at her reluctant nod, Kaden stepped up to the desk. He had no intention of walking away. He would watch Greg's every move. If the man deleted anything, Kaden would see it.

"Do you like my computer, Francesca?" Greg taunted over his shoulder. "It makes running a ranch so much faster and easier."

Kaden refused to take his eyes off Greg, though he detested the man for speaking to Frankie in such a way.

Was that Greg's plan? To make Kaden look away so he could delete the footage unnoticed?

Kaden could see why Frankie distrusted the man. He was sly.

"Just get the video," she said.

Greg chuckled, but he was able to remove the SD card and insert it into his PC. The files began to transfer. "Feel free to use my satellite phone to call your family," he said to Kaden.

Kaden felt Frankie's gaze on him, and it took every ounce of strength not to make eye contact with her. To do so would mean letting Greg go unsupervised. Had his invitation to use the phone been deliberate?

"I'll wait until after," Kaden replied. "I want to see who hit my plane."

"Suit yourself." Greg clicked the arrow to play the recording. "Here he is."

An older man with gray hair was seen holding the drone. He turned it over a few times before he set it down. Then the image showed nothing but grass.

"Go back," Frankie said, her eyes narrowing.

"Do you know him?" Kaden asked.

She shook her head. "I don't think so. But I want to see him again."

Greg rewound the recording to the beginning and hit *Play* again.

Leo started to bark and ran to the door.

Chris was stepping inside. "Sit," he ordered, and the animal slunk away. "Francesca! What do you think you're doing?"

The man appeared disheveled and angry. His white hair stood on end, and his eyes bulged, but his anger stalled when he saw the computer screen.

Chris stepped back and nearly crumpled to the floor, as though someone had punched him in the stomach. "What is this? Where did you get this?"

Francesca moved toward her father with her arms extended to help him. "It's the person whose drone hit Kaden's plane. We found it under the plane. Papa, you're not well. Let me help you."

Chris waved her hand away. "He's here," he rasped.

"Who's here?" Frankie asked. She followed her father's stare to the man on the computer screen. "Do you know who this man is?"

Chris lifted a trembling hand to her cheek. "Oh, Francesca. I tried to protect you, but I've failed." His hand dropped to her wrist. "We have to go. Right now."

She dug in her heels. "Papa, tell me what is going on. Who is this man? What were you protecting me from? I deserve to know."

Chris's eyes filled with tears, and Kaden actually felt sorry for the man. It seemed that whatever decisions he had made decades before were coming back to haunt him. But Frankie didn't deserve to pay for her father's choices.

"Is Frankie in danger?" Kaden asked in a low tone that left no room for any more lies.

Chris glanced at the screen. Greg had paused the video and zoomed in on the face. The man on-screen had eyes that appeared vacant of any feeling. Did the stranger care that he could have killed someone?

Either way, Frankie would not be his next victim.

Kaden stepped away from the desk, giving up his scrutiny of Greg in favor of protecting Frankie. "Listen, I don't know what this is all about, but I have known since I landed on this property that something isn't right. There are a lot of secrets in this place, but I personally don't care about any of them. All I do care about is Frankie's safety. Is she safe here?" he asked Chris.

"It doesn't matter. I'm not going anywhere," Frankie interjected, reaching her free hand toward Kaden.

And the image of her father gripping one of her arms, while she held out the other to him, merely proved his point more.

"Let me handle this, Kaden," she said.

He didn't take her hand. It would mean linking himself to Chris Stiles, and he wanted nothing to do with the man.

"Who is the man on the computer screen?" Kaden asked Chris. "If you won't tell me, at least tell Frankie. Be honest with her. She deserves to know who she's up against. Will he try to hurt her—or worse?"

The sole response in the room was Frankie's sharp inhale.

Chris didn't even blink. When he spoke, his voice sent a chill through Kaden. "Boy, you don't know what you're dealing with. I see you got your plane out of the water. It would be best if you hightail it out of here while you still can. Let's go, Francesca." He tugged on his daughter's arm.

"Wait." She pulled back but didn't break the hold. "Answer his question."

"Not here."

Frankie opened her mouth to protest, then closed it again and moved with her father toward the door.

"Frankie, I need to know if you're safe here," Kaden called to her at the door.

Her smile was anything but reassuring, but her head was held high. She was a strong woman, but he wanted her to know she didn't have to face the situation alone.

Yet the words remained locked up inside him. How could he promise such a thing when he planned to move out as fast as possible, and she wouldn't fly out with him?

As though she could read his mind, she said, "I'm not your problem, but thank you for your concern."

She walked out with her father, and soon he heard the truck engine come to life. The crunch of gravel beneath the tires grated on his senses until the sound disappeared into the distance.

Kaden turned to Greg and the frozen image of the man on the screen behind him.

The farm and any past drama surrounding it might not have been his problem, but he wouldn't leave until he felt sure Frankie would be all right. "Tell me everything you know about Frankie's mother."

Greg averted his gaze. "I don't know anything about her."

"You're lying," Kaden said evenly. "Was she killed?"

"I don't know. I suppose it's possible."

"Or?" Kaden prompted.

Greg raised his head to stare intently at Kaden. "Or Vera Stiles never existed in the first place."

Frankie sat beside her father in silence as he pulled up to their home. He'd yet to answer any of her questions, but she gave him the time to calm down. She had never seen him so frightened. To Kaden,

Papa may have come off as angry, but she knew him better. Fear was what drove him and prevented him from making rational decisions.

"Grab a few pieces of clothing. Nothing but basic necessities," he said as he shut off the engine and climbed out. The way he surveyed their property suggested that he was searching for someone lurking in the shadows.

"Papa, I'm not leaving our farm. I meant what I said to Kaden. I'm not going anywhere."

"Francesca, you don't know what you're saying." He started toward the house.

She rushed from the truck to go after him. "I would if you had been honest with me, instead of keeping me in the dark my whole life. Papa, are you listening to me?" She reached his side, but her father barreled straight ahead as if he hadn't even heard her. "Talk to me, please."

"Do as you're told and pack a bag. Every second counts if you want to stay alive."

Papa's words stunned her more. She'd never heard him speak in such a foreboding manner. Frankie stood in the living room and tried to gather her thoughts. Papa hurried to his room, and she watched him through the open door, taking down an old leather satchel from his closet shelf. His movements were frantic, and what he threw into the bag seemed haphazard. He clearly wasn't thinking rationally.

Frankie slowly approached his room and leaned against the doorframe, her heart breaking at the sight of her father in such dire straits. "Please tell me what's happening. You're scaring me."

"Apparently not enough, because you're wasting time fussing over me instead of packing." Papa moved down to the next drawer.

"I'm not going to pack." She stepped into his room and caught his hands to get his attention. "This is my farm. My whole life you've told me it will be mine someday. I will not give it up, not for anyone."

Papa's shoulders sagged. "I have to keep you safe."

"From whom?"

He shook his head. "Francesca, I've done things. Bad things."

"Tell me."

"I can't. You wouldn't understand. You would hate me."

"Never. You're my father, and nothing will change that."

"This will change everything. We have to go. Before it's too late."

"Go if you must, but I won't be leaving with you. I'm ready to take over the farm completely."

"I know. You were ready when you were sixteen." He smiled and squeezed her hand, then took a deep breath. "I'm probably going to regret this, but we'll stay if that's what you really want. You're right. This is our land, and we will defend it as long as we can."

"Why do we have to defend it at all, Papa? Who's coming for us, and why? Does this person have anything to do with my mother?"

"He's my enemy, and yes. I lost her because of him."

"So her death wasn't an accident. Who *is* he?"

Papa closed his eyes. "He's someone who should have stayed buried. He should have stayed where I put him."

7

*K*aden remained at Greg's overnight, and the next morning, the two men moved the plane to his barn to work on it. Greg rode his ATV alongside the aircraft as Kaden navigated carefully over the terrain. He taxied it up to the double doors and then inside, where Greg had cleared a large area to serve as a makeshift hangar. Greg had all the current equipment, but in the end, all Kaden needed was the paintless dent repair kit he kept in the plane.

Kaden still didn't trust Greg, but he appreciated the help. The work took his mind off his worries for Frankie as well.

Glancing in the direction of her farm, he wondered if she was still there. The way Chris had dragged her out of Greg's house the night before, Kaden wouldn't have been surprised if father and daughter had skipped town. It had been clear that Chris was deathly afraid of the owner of the drone, whoever he was.

Kaden picked up the drone and tried to find the tail number again. No matter how much he attempted to flatten out the mangled plastic, he couldn't make out the numbers that had once been there. It was as if they'd been purposely removed. The owner didn't want to be tracked down, which likely meant he was up to no good. He could have been searching for something or someone on the farm's back acreage. The thought made Kaden want to go back out to the lake and figure out what the stranger had wanted to find. Kaden would consider the possibility that the drone had targeted him directly, but Chris seemed to have history with the man, whereas Kaden did not.

"How's the plane coming?" Greg stepped inside the barn with a satellite phone.

"I think she's as good as I'll get her. Once I get to Alaska, I'll take her in to the professionals for a full tune-up."

"Are you sure she's safe to fly?"

"No I'm not, but I don't have a choice."

"Sure, you do." Greg held up the phone. "Your parents would help you."

Kaden grimaced at the phone. "I suppose I've kept them waiting far too long."

"They're probably planning your funeral."

Kaden's scoff fell flat as he considered that there might be some truth to Greg's statement. "If my radio transmission went through, they would've been notified that I'm alive. If it didn't, they might have come to look for me if they cared enough to do so."

"I guess you'll find out when you call them," Greg said and passed the phone over to Kaden, giving him directions on how to use it. Greg left the barn to give Kaden some privacy.

Kaden made the call to his father and was about to hang up after numerous rings when, finally, he answered.

"This is Malcolm Phillips," his father said in his snooty business tone.

"Dad? It's me. I don't know if you heard, but I had to make an emergency landing. I'm in Washington state."

Silence ensued on the other end, and after a deep sigh, his dad replied, "Yes, we were notified your plane went off the radar. Your message transmitted that you were safe, so we knew you were alive. Were you hurt?"

"Not really. Got a bump on the head but was fine by morning. Never lost consciousness or anything." Kaden waited to see if his father would ask about the plane. It was a sore subject between them.

His parents had never approved of his purchase or his plan to use it. Their support was only extended to ventures that might benefit them.

"When can we expect you home?"

Kaden studied his plane, which was mercifully ready to be flown again. "There wasn't much damage to the wing. I think I've repaired it sufficiently enough to get me to the rest of the way to Alaska."

More silence. "I see. Your mother will be upset. She was hoping to see you with her own two eyes to know that you are okay."

"I think it's best if I keep moving forward. I plan to test the plane today and be on my way soon after. I'll call you when I get to Alaska and let you know I made it there safely." Kaden left out what he really wanted to say. *If Mom wanted to see me with her own two eyes, she's had three days to get to Washington.*

"All right. Have you spoken to Julia since you left?"

An image of Julia Woodworth passed into Kaden's mind. Marriage to the billionaire heiress of a Silicon Valley tech company had been something his parents were happy to support.

"I haven't spoken to her since she broke off the engagement. Why do you ask?"

"We've been speaking with her, and she would like to talk to you. I think with a little finesse and dedication, Julia could be persuaded to give your relationship another try."

"Dad, our relationship will never work. I need you to understand this."

"All I'm asking is that you give her a call. Is that so hard to do? After all, she was someone you planned to spend the rest of your life with."

No, you *planned for me to spend the rest of my life with her.*

Why was saying what was on his mind so difficult? Why couldn't he stick up for himself with his father? Why was he already recalling Julia's phone number in his mind as though he would hang up with his father and dial her next?

"I really don't have the time. I have too much to do to get the plane up in the air. Perhaps when I get to Alaska, I'll find a few minutes."

The silence extended so long that Kaden thought his father had hung up on him.

"Dad? Are you still there?"

"You know very well that if you get to Alaska, Julia will never speak to you again. I'm beginning to think that's what you want."

"Not at all. I've known Julia my whole life. She's a friend and always will be. But we want different things, so a life together doesn't make sense for us. She wants California. I want Alaska." *And you want her money.*

Once again, Kaden bit his tongue to stop himself from saying what was really on his mind. His father would never admit the truth anyway.

"Well, I have another call coming in. I'm glad you're all right. We'll be in touch."

"Okay, bye," Kaden responded, but he knew his father was already gone.

A lump in his throat made swallowing nearly impossible. He held the phone so tight that he heard it creak, and put it down on the workbench before he broke it.

"That bad, huh?" Greg stepped back into the barn, obviously having overheard all or part of the conversation.

"I'm not the person they want me to be. I barely passed the bar for my law license."

"I never had kids myself, but I had a dad. Sometimes we think they're bossing us around, but it's simply their flawed way of showing they care about us. It's not until we're out on our own, making ends meet, that we realize they were just trying to save us from making the same mistakes they did. Of course, by then it's too late for them to help, and you have to figure out how to make it on your own."

The urge to let himself be persuaded by Greg's surprisingly insightful words pulled hard. But knowing the man had been a thorn in Frankie's side for so long held Kaden back from falling for any ploy Greg might have to get Kaden on his side.

"Is that what you've been doing with Frankie all this time? Figuring out how you'll make it out here on your own? I see your land is dried up, and you need water. What did your dad think when you bought this property?"

Greg's jaw clenched but he answered the question. "He was against it. Said I would regret it until the day I die."

"And have you?"

"Not yet. I'm not ready to give up. As long as I have breath in my body, I'll find a way to make something of this ranch."

"Well, try to find a way that doesn't involve Frankie."

Kaden knew Greg didn't like being told what to do, but Kaden couldn't leave without warning the man to keep his distance from her. To say nothing would plague his conscience forever, and Kaden meant to hit the skies with a clear head.

"Since your plane is ready, I suggest you get going," Greg said.

"I suppose I wasn't expecting a friendly farewell. I have one more stop to make, and then I'll be gone. I do appreciate the help you've given me, and I really do hope you figure out a way to make your ranch thrive. It's an amazing piece of property. It would be a shame for it to go under."

"Never. No matter what I have to do, I'll keep it going."

Greg's words sat uneasily with Kaden as he taxied out of the barn and lifted off. He stayed low to test the wing. Feeling confident the plane would be safe to fly, he gained a little more altitude and flew across Greg's ranch over to Frankie's farm. When he reached her land, he brought the plane down on a long flat area near the barn. He pulled up alongside the structure and shut down the aircraft.

After exiting the cockpit, he passed by the open doors to the barn and noticed her horses were not in their stalls. The truck was also missing. He rapped on the front door of the house and peeked in through the windows. The place was shut up completely and tightly secured. In the few days that Kaden had been there, Frankie had never locked up.

Something was wrong.

Whoever had been on that camera had scared Chris into running. But what had her father said to Frankie to make her go with him?

Frankie sat at her mother's memorial out by the lake. Kaden's plane was gone, and she had to assume he had taken it to Greg's ranch. For all she knew, he could be long gone.

She hated the way their time together had ended. Even knowing him for a few days had left a lasting impact on her. She would have liked to say goodbye, would have liked to thank him for opening her eyes. Without Kaden, she would not have been able to visit her mother's memorial cross. The night his plane had come down was the night her life had taken a turn. For so long that area of her property had terrified her.

But no longer. Nothing would scare her from any piece of her own land again. Even if Papa begged her to abandon it.

She heard a horse approaching and twisted around to see her father riding Blossom toward her. Her own horse was tethered to the willow tree, munching on the tall grass. Frankie had convinced her father to stay the night before, but he woke that morning with a need to comb the back forty acres. He worried the man on the drone's camera might be back there.

The fact that Papa had brought his gun concerned her more.

Would he kill someone?

Francesca, I've done things. Bad things.

His words from the previous night filtered through her mind and into her dreams. He'd yet to explain himself or tell her who the man on the camera was. All she knew was that the white-haired stranger was connected to her mother in some way.

Frankie reread the inscription on the cross—*Till Death Do Us Part.*

"Why did you carve that on my mother's memorial?" she asked as Papa stepped out of the saddle and wrapped his reins around a branch.

"To remind me of the vow I took."

"But she died. That means the vow is over."

"It will never be over for me. As long as I live, Vera will be my wife." He knelt beside Frankie and showed her four black pieces of plastic. "I found these."

Frankie took the pieces from him. "You found more of the drone. Papa, we have to find Kaden and get these to him. He'll need them for an investigation into who hit his plane."

"If you care about that boy, you will never see him again." Papa's voice held no room for negotiation.

"But he needs these."

"The owner of that drone is not a man Kaden wants to find. Trust me on this." Papa took back the pieces and put them in a pile in front of him. "I didn't see any other signs of someone being out here. I'm not sure how far this drone can go away from its controller before it's out of range. Perhaps he navigated it from the mountains or even further."

"And you still won't tell me who he is." Frankie watched her father's face for any sign of giving in.

"Your safety is my sole concern. If you won't leave with me, then I'll have to prepare for his arrival."

"You really think he'll come here?"

"The drone proves he already has. He can't leave any stone unturned. He will hunt everywhere until he finds me. Until he finds you."

"And then what?"

Papa took her hand. She studied his weathered and wrinkled skin. For twenty-five years he'd worked the land, making a home for her, keeping her in isolation.

Why? What had he done that would call for such a decision?

"Then we fight to stay alive." He reached into his pocket and passed a revolver to her. "I know you can fire the shotgun, but I need you to practice on a closer target. I'll do my best to be on guard before you have to use this, but there's only one of me, and he will come with reinforcements."

Frankie whispered, "How do you know that?"

"Because I used to be one of his reinforcements."

Francesca, I've done things. Bad things.

She handed the gun back to her father, still trying to process his words. "Papa, I have to ask you something, and I need you to tell me the truth." Frankie's mouth went dry as she deliberated the necessity of having her question answered against what it might do to her relationship with her father. Did she really want to know the answer? Taking a deep breath, she blurted, "Did you kill Mama?"

Her father's hand tightened around hers. "Not in the way you might be thinking. But I know I broke her heart."

Frankie scanned the area, stopping at the lake that had scared her and kept her at bay for so many years. "Did . . . did she take her own life?"

Papa shook his head. "Don't do this to yourself, Francesca. Vera is dead to us, and she must remain so."

Frankie pulled her hand away. "Greg knows. He knows what you did. Why does our neighbor know more about you than your own daughter does?"

"Does he now?" Papa raised an eyebrow toward Greg's ranch. "I'll have to pay him a visit and make sure he knows your safety comes first."

"I can take care of myself." She grabbed the broken drone pieces, then stormed over to her horse and swung into the saddle. Frankie glared down at her father, struggling to hold back her anger. "I don't know who you are anymore. You say I have an enemy coming, but you won't tell me anything that could actually help me prepare for his arrival. So I have to consider the possibility that I'm looking right at him."

Papa lifted a hand to her. "I'm trying to protect you. That's all I've ever done."

"The thing that's most likely to get me killed is the knowledge you've kept from me. You underestimate me by assuming I can't handle the truth. And now I see you always have." With that, she kicked in her heels and rode back toward her farmhouse. She wondered if her father ever planned on relinquishing Nighthawk Farm to her control. Had it all been lip service to convince her to stay? If everything about his life was a lie, then she had to assume everything he ever said to her was as well.

She rode fast with the afternoon sun in her eyes as she headed toward the western portion of her land—not that it felt appropriate to call it hers after the events of the last few days. By the time she made it back to the barn, her blood was boiling, and she galloped Shadow inside, then came to an abrupt halt at the sight of Kaden's aircraft.

"Kaden?" She jumped down from the saddle, searching the inside of the barn but coming up empty. She ran toward the house and saw him coming around the side. Without a thought, she raced into his arms and buried her face in his neck, where she burst into the tears that had built since she left her father. The wails coming out of her mouth muffled against the soft fabric of his denim shirt. "He killed her, Kaden. Papa killed my mother."

Kaden pulled back and gripped her face. "Are you sure?"

"He may not have been the one to do it, but he caused it. All these years, I thought it was an accident, but he knew the truth the whole time and hid it from me. He all but admitted that my mother is dead because of him. I can't stay here any longer. Take me with you. Please." She sounded desperate even to her own ears. It was a foreign sensation after a lifetime of feeling sure of herself. But everything about her was a lie. She was nothing but a captive, and she wouldn't stay in her prison another night.

"If that's what you want, we can be out of here in an hour."

Frankie nodded and swiped at the tears on her cheeks. "I won't be long." To think that the night before, she had watched her father pack a bag even as she had refused to, and suddenly it was all she wanted.

She raced inside, toward the back corner of the house, where her once-cozy room felt like a jail cell. She didn't own any luggage but had a backpack she'd used in college. She stuffed it with a few pairs of jeans, some shirts, a couple of pairs of shoes, and other necessities. On her way out the door, she grabbed her cowboy hat from the dresser and donned it. The one photo she had of her mother was tucked into the corner of the dresser's mirror. It had been taken when Frankie was a few months old. Vera held her daughter close and smiled beautifully at the camera. Frankie tucked it into the backpack. Passing through the living room, she snatched her ledger off the desk. She knew she wouldn't need it, but she also refused to leave all her hard work behind to benefit a man who'd deceived her for her entire life.

When she stepped out to the porch, she heard Kaden in the barn, getting the plane ready for takeoff. She scanned the trees, expecting to see her father riding in. He couldn't be far behind, and she knew he would try to stop her.

Her eyes narrowed on something strange, but it wasn't Papa. Out past the trees, she could see black smoke curling into the sky.

"Fire!"

8

*A*t the sound of Frankie's scream, Kaden sprinted out of the barn and spotted the billowing smoke above the tree line. "Where's the truck?" he called to Frankie.

"Papa hid it in the trees behind the barn. I'll get it." Frankie dashed off with her backpack and soon returned with the old vehicle. "Get in!"

He jumped into the passenger seat as she took off, heading east. "I think the fire is coming from Greg's. Maybe the barn?" Kaden thought about how his plane had been in there a couple of hours ago.

"The poor horses." Frankie murmured, and the rest of the way was filled with a tense silence in the cabin. The only sound came from the old truck clanging as it hit ruts in the packed dirt path. A few times, Kaden thought the truck would come apart.

Frankie pulled into a long gravel drive that led to the ranch house. The house seemed fine, but the barn was ablaze. Greg was nowhere in sight, and the barn doors were still closed.

"I have to get the horses," Frankie said, jumping from the truck.

"Wait. It's not safe to go in there." Kaden followed her, knowing nothing would stop her from trying to save the animals. When they reached the doors, he used his denim shirt to lift the metal latch.

Immediately, flames licked out at them. He squinted through the smoke to see the horses within, whinnying in distress on the other side of the arena.

"Stay low," he said, and guided Frankie inside with an arm out to shield her face. They reached the first stall and as he lifted the door, she reached for the horse's mane. Thankfully, the horse allowed Frankie to guide her outside. By the time Frankie made it back, Kaden had opened the next stall and passed the horse to her.

"There's one more," Frankie called, pointing behind him. She coughed, and he knew he couldn't let her back inside the barn.

"I'll get the horse. Get outside and watch the others. Don't come back, okay?"

She held tight to the mane of the horse she held and pressed her face into the horse's neck to keep from breathing in more smoke. He turned back and saw that the flames had moved closer to the stall door.

The horse bucked against the door and the walls of the stall. He wouldn't go peacefully like the last two. The animal wanted out, and there was a good chance he would trample anyone who stood in his way. But as sweat poured from his forehead in the fiery inferno, Kaden knew he couldn't walk away. He would have to risk it.

Dodging flames to his right, he pressed himself against the wall and slunk low toward the stall.

"Whoa, boy. I'm going to get you out of here, but you need to be calm or we're both done for." Kaden put a hand through the bars for the horse to approach him. He could see the whites of the animal's eyes and knew the poor creature was petrified. "I don't blame you," Kaden said as he felt the skin on his back heating up.

He pushed his hand through further and touched the horse's nose. The animal jerked back, then returned. "There you go. I'm not going to hurt you."

Slowly, Kaden lifted the latch and pulled the door wide, putting his hand back inside for the horse to feel reassured. Keeping his voice low, he coaxed the animal out of the stall, but the fire stopped the horse cold.

"It's just a little bit farther. Stay with me, buddy." Kaden stood in front of the horse and pulled on its neck, forcing him to move along the wall until finally, they both broke free from the barn. The horse took off into the pasture and over the hills.

There was no sign of Frankie. He headed toward the house and saw the front door left open. Stepping inside, he called her name, but there was no response. The truck was still there, so he knew she hadn't left. So then where was she?

Leo sprinted into the living room and did circles around Kaden. The dog barked, and Kaden noticed his nose was red with blood. But whose? The German Shepherd didn't seem to be injured.

"Frankie, where are you?" Kaden moved into the kitchen and stopped cold.

"I'm here." Frankie knelt over Greg, who was sprawled on the floor, unmoving.

Kaden was certain that Greg was dead. He appeared to have been shot.

"We need to step back. There's nothing you can do for him." Kaden touched Frankie's shoulder. "We'll call the police, but we need to leave. Now."

Frankie shook her head. "Papa did this. I told him that Greg knew about his past. He must have come here and killed our neighbor. Papa said he would pay Greg a visit to make sure I was kept safe. But his idea of keeping me safe is to make people disappear. First my mother, and now Greg."

"We don't know that for sure. The police will figure it out. Let's go."

Slowly, Frankie raised her gaze to meet his. "What kind of monster is my father?"

Kaden didn't have an answer for that either. He knew the man was overprotective, but Chris would have to be downright malicious to commit such a heinous crime. Kaden held his hand out to help her up and was grateful when she took it.

Wrapping an arm around her shoulders, he led her out of the house onto the porch. Leo followed them out, whining anxiously.

"Sit on the steps," Kaden instructed her, then ducked back inside for the satellite phone. As he dialed, he thought of how Greg had made him call his parents a couple of short hours ago, sharing unexpected wisdom as he did.

And now he was dead.

Kaden called emergency services and informed them about the fire and Greg's demise. "Please hurry," he begged the dispatcher before hanging up. The murderer couldn't be far away and might return. If Chris were the guilty party, Kaden didn't doubt that he would be the next victim.

"I—I did this," Frankie stammered through her trembling.

Kaden sat beside her on Greg's porch bench, with his arm around her, pulling her in close. But no matter how tight he held her, she shivered as if she were freezing. All she could see in her mind's eye was Greg's lifeless body.

"You did not shoot Greg, so that can't possibly be your fault. But you did save the horses, in spite of what I said. I'm proud of you, Frankie. You are so brave. Braver than I have ever been."

"You went in too."

"Because of you." He chuckled, but she could tell he was as scared as she was.

"I'm so sorry you have to deal with this. All you wanted was to go to Alaska and live your life on your own terms."

"It's okay. I'm glad I'm here with you. I'm sorry you had to find Greg like that."

She faced him. "Papa had a gun. When we were out at the lake, he tried to give it to me, but I didn't want it. If I had taken it, Greg would still be alive."

"You can't know that. First, there's no evidence that your father did this. I really hope he didn't."

"Who else could have? There's no one out here for miles. Papa said he was coming here. And he's been acting weird ever since he saw that man on the screen. He wanted to run last night, but I told him I would never leave my farm." Frankie let out a sob. "Why didn't I go with him? Then Greg would still be alive."

Kaden's arms tightened around her fully, and she buried her face in his neck. As much as she wished for his sake that he had left already, she was so glad he was there with her. She couldn't imagine facing such horror alone. The three days she'd known him felt like a lifetime. It was so strange how a tragedy brought strangers closer. But even before the fire and finding Greg dead on the floor, there was something about Kaden that made him feel like a kindred spirit.

Frankie lifted her face and searched his eyes, so full of compassion and worry.

"How far are the police from here?" he asked.

"At least thirty minutes." She glanced toward the barn, which was fully engulfed in flames. All that could be done was to let it burn out and pray it didn't spread.

"I don't think it's safe to sit here. Whoever shot Greg could come back."

Frankie inhaled sharply at the thought. "We can't go back to my house either."

Kaden led her off the porch and around the back of the house where a small shed leaned against the wall. He opened the door carefully and searched inside, then signaled that it was safe. She followed him inside. Before he closed the door, Frankie saw Leo, forlorn in the tall grass. He whined, and she called him. The dog looked back at the house before trotting over to them and letting them close him inside the shed with them. He huddled against Frankie's leg, and she murmured soothingly to him, trying to infuse him with a calm she didn't feel.

There was nothing to do but wait.

Wait for the police.

Wait for her father.

Wait for death to find them.

Kaden handed her a shovel while he held a pitchfork, and the two sat in the middle of the shed with Leo at their side.

An eternity stretched before they finally heard sirens off in the distance. Frankie didn't dare let her guard down and still held her breath until the first responders arrived.

Kaden stood first and went to the door. Opening it slowly, he revealed three police cruisers, a fire truck, and an ambulance on the lawn. Only then did Frankie let out the breath she had been holding.

Putting down the farm tools, they approached the police together to pass along what little they knew. The paramedics wrapped blankets around them to ward against shock. An officer stepped out of the house with a piece of paper in his gloved hands.

"The house is clear, but I found a note," he said to his superior.

"What does it say?" the lead investigator asked.

"'There is no place you can hide that I won't find you. Or your little girl.'" He passed the note to the investigator. "Did the victim have any children?"

"No," Kaden responded. "I spoke with him earlier today, and he specifically mentioned never having kids. That letter wasn't meant for Greg."

"So Papa didn't do this," Frankie said, relief washing through her.

"It seems not, but then who did?" he asked. "Who is your father running from?"

Frankie recalled her father's fear. After seeing Greg murdered, she understood why he was so afraid.

"He's been hiding from a monster," she said. "And they've tracked him down. We have to find him before they do."

"But Frankie, it's not just him they want." Kaden peered into her eyes. "They want you too."

9

On Wednesday afternoon, Detective Burke stood in the middle of Frankie's kitchen after completing a thorough examination of the property. Kaden stood off to the side against the wall and watched Frankie fold in on herself as the detective informed her that he'd found no sign of her father. Chris hadn't returned to the house the previous night, so Frankie hadn't seen him since she'd left him at the lake the day before. With Greg's murder and the warning letter to Chris, every minute he was absent increased her worry.

"What about the drone?" Frankie asked. "Can you track down who owns it? Find him, and we'll find my father."

The investigator explained, "The drone has a tracking device on it, but we can only tell its location, not who the owner is. And without a serial number, all we have to go by is the video. I believe that if you'd brought the drone here to your house instead of Greg Mullen's, he might still be alive. The evidence indicates that the killer tracked the device to Mr. Mullen's house."

The weight of that statement lingered in the room. If the killer had come to the Stileses' home first, Frankie would be dead, and she would never have seen it coming, like Greg hadn't. The thought made Kaden's stomach clench.

"Is there any place on the property that your father would have gone? Perhaps he's hiding out somewhere?" Burke suggested.

Frankie dropped her forehead into her hand. "I don't know of any place. He had his horse, so I suppose he could have gone up into the mountains. I hope he did. The alternative is unthinkable." Her voice cracked, and Kaden stepped forward to touch her shoulder. She put her hand on his and held on. "The truth is, I didn't spend much time out by the lake, so I don't know what's out there."

"Do you have a map?"

"Papa had a few old maps of the property." Frankie stood and went through the door. Kaden heard her rummaging through the desk, and then she returned with an old trifold map, which she spread on the table.

"This is all your property?"

"Yes, this is Nighthawk Farm."

"That's an interesting name for an orchard. Did your father name it, or did it come with that name?" Burke bent over the map.

"As far as I know, Papa came up with the name with my mother before she died—when they first moved here and bought the land. There was a kettle of nighthawks that roosted on the fence posts and fed on insects over the lake. I always assumed that's where the name came from."

"Interesting," Burke said. "What I know about them is they know how to camouflage. They could be sitting right in the grass in front of you and you wouldn't know until you were on top of them. They hide in plain sight and can sit motionless for hours. But when they feed, they dive straight down, swoop in for the kill, and skyrocket right back up to disappear into the night."

Frankie's silence made Kaden wonder what she was thinking. Her whole world was coming apart at the seams and even the name of her farm held a hidden meaning. Was Chris himself the nighthawk for which his farm was named? Was he hiding in plain sight as they spoke, waiting for his prey to get close enough that he could swoop in and take them out? Or was he running scared, as the prey himself?

Kaden didn't know, and he didn't care. All that mattered to him was getting Frankie to a safe place.

"I'd like to fly Frankie out of here today," he said to the investigator. "She's not safe on this farm."

Burke lifted his head from poring over the map. "That plane has not been cleared to fly, and I still have questions that she needs to answer. You're not going anywhere." He dropped his gaze back to the drawing in front of him. His finger traced a few lines around the lake and into the mountains. "This appears to be an old mine. Do you know anything about the area?"

Frankie shook her head. "I've never been up there. I always stayed away from the back forty. Papa said it was too dangerous and I could get hurt, like Mama. That was enough for me to avoid it."

"And what exactly happened to your mother?"

"That seems to be the question of the week. I was always told her death was an accident. That she had drowned in the lake right after they moved here. Papa put up a memorial out there, but that's all I know."

Kaden stationed himself behind Frankie. He hesitated to give the information that Greg had shared with him because it would likely shake Frankie even more, but it couldn't be helped. The police had to know as much as he could tell them. "When I spoke to Greg yesterday, he led me to believe that Vera Stiles never existed."

Frankie swung around with a look of shock on her face. "Why would you say such a thing? I was born, wasn't I?"

"I'm not sure if he meant it that way. I got the impression that Vera was never on the farm. Greg never met her or even saw her off in the distance. If that's the case, your father lied about any accident."

"Says Greg."

"And now he's dead. How convenient." Kaden let that little fact end the conversation.

Frankie's face reddened, but he considered that better than the ashen complexion she'd had since she found Greg's body. "My father did not kill him. You saw the letter."

"Which he could've written himself to throw the police off his trail. He was ready to leave the night before. He could have killed Greg and then ridden into the mountains."

"My father wouldn't leave me," she said firmly. "At least not without saying goodbye."

Kaden was saved from having to reply when Burke pointed to a spot on the map and said, "I'll get a team together to search around this location. It could be an old mine or a cave. Either way, Chris could be hiding out in there."

"I'll go with you," Kaden said.

Frankie cut in, "Not without me. I'm going too."

Detective Burke folded up the map. "Let's get started while we still have daylight. But be careful out there. Our killer won't have gone far."

The opening ended up being a cave. Even though it was a hot summer afternoon, the interior felt cold and wet. Frankie figured it became an ice cave each winter. When she, Kaden, Detective Burke, and two other officers made their way through the narrow opening, she felt a breeze hit her face from deeper inside.

"There must be another entrance," she said, flicking on her flashlight to search for evidence of another human presence.

She found plenty of claw marks on the stones made by bears, mountain lions, and even roosting bats. The sound of water dripping down the walls told her the stream went somewhere, and she used her light to follow it. As the cave declined, the water trickled along the edges, growing deeper and faster. Eventually, their steps became more difficult with no railing to hold onto. The sound of rushing water guided her until she could trek no further. The water swept into a waterfall and thundered into a black pit. It wasn't what she'd expected to find in the cave.

"A dead end," Detective Burke said. "I'd really like to see a map or satellite image of this whole place, if one was ever made. I'll have to check public records to find out. Let's head back and I'll try to locate one. It's too late tonight, but if I find another opening, we can start tomorrow."

Frankie stood on the precipice. Had her father come the same way? Would he have jumped into the water below? As she turned to follow the team's retreating backs, she caught sight of something on a sharp rock. She bent to examine it and found a rope tied around the rock and trailing in the fast-moving water.

Someone had been there and used the rope to descend over the waterfall.

"Detective?" she called, but no one answered.

She shifted toward the exit, but slipped and dropped her flashlight. As she scrambled to right herself, she saw the flashlight bobbing away on the current. Without thinking, she ran after it, hoping to catch it before it disappeared into oblivion.

She didn't reach it in time, and the light bounced crazily as it toppled over the waterfall. That was when she realized how close she'd come to the edge, and she tried to stop, only to topple over into the cold water. Her hand slid across the wet rock, scrabbling for purchase, and she felt her legs fall over the rocky face.

Before she could scream for help, someone caught her and pulled her back in the nick of time, then let go of her.

"Kaden? Thank you so much. I almost went over," she said breathlessly into the pitch-dark. She pushed herself to her knees.

Her arms shook in fear and fatigue as she carefully rose upright. "I can't see a thing. Can you put your flashlight on?"

"Frankie?" Kaden's voice called from a distance, sending a frigid tremor through her body. If Kaden hadn't pulled her up, then who had?

"Papa?" she whispered. "Is that you? You don't have to hide. You're not in any trouble. Please, come back with me. I've been so worried."

A sound echoed to her left.

"Papa," she said a little louder, but no response came. If he had been there, he was gone again.

Frankie scooted forward, against the flow of water. One wrong move and she would plummet to her death. Feeling her way along the craggy rock, she crawled to stay low and secure.

Kaden called to her again, and she wondered briefly whether he had purposefully let her fall behind. She shouldn't have let herself get so angry at what Kaden had insinuated. Simply because Greg had never seen her mother didn't mean Vera Stiles hadn't been real.

Frankie hit the wall and bumped her head with a groan. Then she heard another sound coming up behind her. Someone or something was following her. Was it an animal?

"You can run, but you can't hide." A low voice behind startled her so much, she slipped.

She was right. She wasn't alone. But it wasn't an animal—at least not the furry kind.

And it definitely wasn't Papa.

Frankie shot to her feet and ran as fast as she could, tripping numerous times and smashing one shoulder into the unforgiving rock wall. She didn't know if she was being followed, and she didn't dare pause to find out.

Just when she didn't think she could make it out, the light of a flashlight blinded her, and she screamed in terror.

"Hey, it's me. It's okay, Frankie. I didn't mean to lose you." It was Kaden.

Frankie gripped his flannel shirt with tight fists. "The killer's in here. We have to get out. Run!"

He grabbed her hand and pulled her along. His light bounced uselessly off the walls and the floor until finally, the opening of the cave showed the moon low in the sky, a beacon.

Together, they burst out into the night to find the officers planning their next move.

"The killer is in there!" Frankie shrieked.

Detective Burke ordered one of the men to escort Kaden and Frankie back to the house and wait for further instruction while he and the other officer checked out the cave.

"That leaves you with one backup," the officer protested.

"I'll take her," Kaden said. "I want her out of here. It's not safe."

Detective Burke took a second to decide but finally agreed. "Get back to the house and stay inside."

Kaden ushered Frankie to the truck. "What happened?"

Frankie rapidly relayed the events in the cave. "There must be another opening, a crevice that he snuck in and out of. I thought he was you at first," she told Kaden. "When I realized you weren't with me, I thought he was Papa. Kaden, I'm sorry about what happened at the house. I shouldn't have been angry with you for telling the truth."

"You have nothing to apologize for." He held the door and watched their surroundings while she climbed in.

Once behind the wheel, Kaden drove as fast as the vehicle would let him. As they neared her farm, she realized she had to leave the place, possibly forever if the police couldn't secure the premises. And what about her father? Would she be leaving Papa behind as well?

"I know I can't stay here, but I feel like I'm running away," she said.

"Not running away. Running to. You're running to safety. You saw what that man did to Greg. It's not safe here."

"He said I could run but I couldn't hide. But if he was going to kill me, why didn't he do it? He had every opportunity. Maybe running isn't such a good idea. I want to know what's going on."

The frown he sent her told her he thought she wasn't thinking clearly. "Is this about your father? He made you so scared to go anywhere that you can't see that this is for your own good."

"I can't leave him behind."

"Frankie, your father is either dead or he left you behind. Can't you see that?"

The brutal truth silenced her for the rest of the ride back. But he was right. Papa had not only left her behind—he'd kept her in the dark her whole life. Surely she owed her father nothing.

"Get inside and stay away from windows," Kaden urged. "I want to check the area outside first, and then I'll be right in."

Frankie headed into the living room and toward the back of the house. In her room, she grabbed her bag, which was still packed from the previous day, and unzipped it to find the photo of her mother atop her belongings. A smiling Vera Stiles held her infant child, which was supposedly Frankie.

Is this photo a lie too?

She zipped the bag again and left her room. Heading back to the living room, she heard a noise from the kitchen. "Kaden?"

"No. Sorry to disappoint," said the voice she knew better than any other.

"Papa!" Frankie dropped the bag and ran to the kitchen.

Her father sat in a chair with his back against the corner of the room. He held the shotgun at the ready, aimed right at her.

"What are you doing?" she demanded, as the hair on the back of her neck stood up.

Papa waved her out of the way and kept the gun trained on the door behind her. Moonlight streamed in through the windows, casting an eerie glow over his face. The dark circles under his eyes and the haunted expression on his face reminded her of a cornered animal.

Frankie took a step forward, hands raised. "Whatever you've done, I know you had a reason. We'll get through this. Right now, we need to help each other stay safe."

Her father lowered the gun as his shoulders sagged in defeat. "It's too late. We've been found, Francesca, and when they get their hands on you, it would be better if you had never been born."

Suddenly, the door slammed against the wall and Kaden shouted, "Get down!"

He tackled her to the ground as a gunshot blasted through the air, shattering glass all around them.

10

The blast echoed in Kaden's ears, and he raised up on his elbows, crunching through shards of glass. It took him a moment to realize the gunshot hadn't come from inside the house. Raising his head, he saw Chris holding his shoulder as he grimaced in pain.

"Papa!" Frankie crawled toward her father.

"Stay there," he ordered, dropping to his knees and out of the window's view. "Kaden, is your plane ready?"

"Yes. I tested it earlier. She can fly."

"Take Francesca out of here and don't let her come back."

"I won't leave without you," Frankie insisted. "You have to come with us. You're hurt."

"He missed on purpose. It was a warning," Chris said sternly. "If he wanted me dead, I would be. Shooting me would be too easy. Now get out of here."

Still Frankie refused to budge, and Kaden knew he couldn't leave Chris there either. Getting to his feet, he raced forward and lifted Chris under his arms. The man cried out in pain, but Kaden's pace didn't falter.

"Get behind the barn," he told Frankie. "Stay low."

Outside, the sound of cars racing down the gravel driveway pushed them forward faster. She scooped up her backpack on her way out and ran as fast as she could while bent double. Kaden stayed right on her heels, dragging Chris along with him.

"Leave me behind," Chris wheezed in Kaden's ear. "I'm slowing you down. I deserve this."

"I won't debate with you there, old man, but I also won't let them do to you what they did to Greg, if only for Frankie's sake." Kaden rushed around the barn and watched Frankie climb into the rear seat of his plane. She helped her father up, and as soon as he was in, Kaden slammed the door shut behind him and sprinted around to fling himself into his seat. The engine fired right up. As he pushed the throttle to put the airplane in motion, close-range gunshots pelted the ground around them.

Kaden took the rutted road as his runway and opened the throttle all the way. Behind him, he could see two black cars chasing them, with men in the front seats sticking guns out the window to take aim at the plane.

"Hurry!" Frankie yelled.

"I hope this works," he said to himself. It was one thing to jump from Greg's land to Frankie's. It was completely different to clear the mountaintops. Once they were airborne, it would be too late to determine whether or not the plane was safe to fly.

"The alternative's death anyway," Chris said, as if he knew what Kaden was thinking.

Frankie kept pressure on her father's wound to try to stop the bleeding, even as she stared wide-eyed through the window at the men following them.

Seconds before they would run out of road and into the trees, Kaden pulled back on the controls to take off. In the distance, he could see Detective Burke's car racing back toward the house. If the detective's vehicle had been any closer, Kaden wouldn't have been able to clear the ground.

"Hey, the shooters are turning around," Frankie said.

"They probably know the police are in that car, and I doubt they want to tangle with them," Chris replied.

Suddenly, the small aircraft wobbled in a patch of turbulence and Frankie gasped. Kaden stabilized the plane and peeked through the window at his damaged wing to see how it was holding up. He felt confident to lift altitude, and soon, the headlights of the cars were specks on the ground below.

"I don't believe it. We made it out," Kaden said.

"Now what?" Frankie called over the small plane's loud engine.

Kaden lifted his headset off its hook and gestured for her to grab the others. Once she'd fitted one over her father's head and donned her own, he said, "I shouldn't have taken off without radioing permission. But to do so now could alert the men below to our destination if they have a scanner. I don't want them knowing we're heading to Alaska."

"We're not," Chris said in a pained voice.

Kaden glanced over his shoulder to find Frankie staring at her father with concern. The older man was bleeding a *lot*. Chris needed medical attention. Would he survive a trip to Alaska?

"Where to then, Chris?" he asked.

"Seattle. Tell the police we need the U.S. Marshals Service."

"What?" Kaden and Frankie shouted at the same time.

The response stunned Kaden so much that the plane dipped. He felt as if he had taken another hit and struggled to regain control of the aircraft. What could Chris possibly need from the U.S. Marshals?

Kaden steadied the plane and forced himself to calm down enough to ask, "What are you into? Because there are only a few reasons you would need to go there, and all of them revolve around organized crime. Believe it or not, I'm an attorney, so I should know. Start explaining yourself, Chris. I won't wait any longer."

"You could have left me behind."

"They would have killed you. I won't have that on my conscience, and I couldn't let Frankie be hurt that way. Now explain yourself.

Who are these men? And who are you?" Kaden caught a glimpse of Frankie's horrified expression. He needed to remember that all of the information of the past few days was new to her too. Detail after horrific detail of her life was revealed, threatening to tear her world apart.

Chris looked at his daughter, and his voice rasped as he spoke. "Everything I've done has been to protect you and prepare you for this day. I know I've been hard on you, Frankie, but I knew at any time you could be left to fend for yourself. I had to know that you would be ready. And you are."

"Ready for what?"

"For when they found me—and killed me."

"You're not going to die. Who found us, Papa?"

"Your mother's family."

Frankie's gasp came through the headsets. "Tell me the truth. Did you kill my mother? Is that why they want you dead?"

Kaden kept his eyes on the dark skies. The conversation happening behind him couldn't lead to anything good. He wanted nothing more than to hold Frankie and force her father to explain everything. But all Kaden could do was fly the plane. He adjusted his flight path to head southwest instead of north, as he knew Frankie was adjusting her own life's direction.

"I didn't kill Vera," Chris said, his voice a harsh, thready whisper. "Nothing killed Vera, because my wife is not dead."

Silence deafened him through the headsets. If Kaden couldn't form words, he imagined Frankie wouldn't be able to either.

Her mother is still alive?

Frankie's mind had to be fragmenting. Her father hadn't merely kept her away from society. He'd kept her away from her own mother. She was likely putting together the same picture. If she couldn't ask the question, then he would.

"Did you kidnap Frankie from her mother?"

Chris dropped his head back on the seat.

"Papa?" Frankie finally spoke in a panic. "Kaden, he's unconscious. He's lost too much blood."

"Keep the pressure on. I'll get us to Seattle as fast as I can." At that point, Kaden had no choice but to radio in his flight plan and hope the men on their tail had no way to pick up the signal. If Chris needed the U.S. Marshals' office to protect them, then the bad guys likely had men in Seattle who could greet them at the airport.

And it wouldn't be to welcome them.

At the same time Frankie had learned her mother was alive, she was in the process of losing her father. Her mind and heart spun as she kept pressure on his wound.

Kaden had asked the question she'd been afraid to. Had Papa kidnapped her when she was an infant? What would cause him to do such a thing? If he didn't regain consciousness, she would never know. And what would happen to her if her mother's family did find her? If she hadn't seen Greg's body with her own eyes, she very well might have run right to them.

Frankie brushed her father's hair from his eyes and wondered if he had taken her because he knew what the family was capable of. But what about her mother? Was Vera Stiles as dangerous as her family?

Frankie thought of the photograph in her bag. The woman in the image held her baby with obvious love and joy.

How could Papa have taken me from a mother who loved me?

"We've been cleared for landing," Kaden said through the headset. "How is he?"

"He still has a pulse. I think the bleeding has stopped, but I don't want to remove my hand to find out."

"No, don't. The paramedics are waiting on the tarmac. And so are the police."

"I hope that keeps these people away so we can get him to the hospital safely."

"Me too."

Minutes later, Kaden brought the plane down smoothly on the runway and taxied around to where various police cars, marked and unmarked, waited with the ambulance. As soon as they came to a stop, the paramedics whisked out a stretcher and pushed it right up to the plane. Kaden opened the door and assisted the paramedics, carefully removing Papa from the plane. Suddenly, Frankie found herself sitting alone and took advantage of the solitude to study her bloodied hands and clothes.

"I've seen enough blood in the last couple of days to last a lifetime," she said to herself. But as long as killers were after them, she wasn't out of the woods.

"Miss Francesca Stiles?" A woman in a black business suit came to the plane's door.

"Yes. Is my father going to be okay?"

"We're taking him to the hospital right now. We have doctors ready to operate. You need to come with us to the facility."

Kaden stepped up behind the woman. "And where are you from?"

The woman put out her hand to shake. "I'm Winnie Perkins. I'm a caseworker with the U.S. Marshals Service. I appreciate you having the police contact us."

"May I ask why my father wanted us to contact you?" Frankie chimed in.

"We'll talk about that in private." She stepped back and offered her hand to help Frankie from the plane.

"I'm a mess."

"That's understandable after what you've been through. Let me help you."

The idea of blood not bothering the woman seemed unfathomable to Frankie. She doubted she would ever get the stain out of her hands, and her clothes were done for.

"Is this your bag?" Winnie asked, hefting her backpack.

"Yes. I didn't bring much, but I'm glad I have some clothes to change into."

"Not to worry. We have plenty of clothes for you to wear at the facility."

It dawned on Frankie that it was the second time the woman had referred to the hospital as "the facility."

"There are clothes for me at the hospital?" Frankie imagined a set of scrubs and wrinkled her nose.

"We're not going to the hospital. We're going to a secure facility. We'll talk in the car, and I'll explain as much as I can." The woman led the way to a black sedan with tinted windows and held the rear door open for Frankie to climb inside. "We have to hurry. It won't be long before you're tracked down."

"Do you know who's after us?"

Winnie nodded to the door and Frankie knew she wouldn't get any more answers until she was inside the car.

"How do I know we can trust you?" Frankie asked.

"Your father told you to contact us. He knows we're your only hope of staying alive."

Frankie looked back at Kaden. "Are you coming?"

"Unfortunately, we can't let him," Winnie responded. "But we will have his plane checked out so he can be on his way."

Frankie stood between the car that would take her to government protection, and Kaden, who would take her to Alaska. And all she wanted was to go home.

"I want Kaden to come with me," she told Winnie firmly. "I'm alive because of him. He tackled me so that I wouldn't be shot. If we leave him here, he'll be in as much danger as we are. You have to keep him safe too. I won't go without him."

Winnie sighed. "This is highly irregular. And it won't be permanent. We've already done a background check on you, Mr. Phillips, so I'll allow you to come to the facility, but that's it. You cannot enter the program unless you can testify on something. However, we won't simply cut you loose and put you at risk either. The office will process you out and help get you someplace safe."

"Thank you. I don't feel comfortable leaving Frankie until I know she's safe."

His words brought disappointment, but Frankie deemed the feeling ridiculous and pushed it aside. Kaden deserved to get on with his life. It was selfish of her to ask him to put his dreams on hold for her, a complete stranger.

Yet they didn't feel like strangers anymore.

After recent events, she would have said that he would be a part of her life forever, even if she never saw him again. But for the time being, she was glad he was still with her. He followed her into the car and took her hand in his.

Winnie climbed into the front passenger seat, and the driver behind the wheel set out for the airport exit.

"We can talk now," Winnie said, twisting in her seat to face them. "I'm surprised your father kept his past a secret from you all this time, and I'm sorry you have to learn about it this way. But under the circumstances, it can't be helped. Francesca, you have some decisions to make about your future."

"What kinds of decisions?" She felt Kaden squeeze her hand.

"Are you familiar with the Witness Security Program run by the U.S. Marshals?"

Beside her, Kaden sucked in a breath between his teeth and growled, "I am."

"Then you know where this conversation is headed," Winnie replied.

"Kaden?" His angry expression confused Frankie. "What is it?"

"I'm thinking your father did you a great disservice." He glared at Winnie. "WITSEC? Seriously?"

At Winnie's nod, he turned to Frankie. The sadness in his eyes nearly made her cry. "Frankie, you're not who you think you are. And your father is not called Chris Stiles. The U.S. Marshals handle witness protection for people who would be in danger if they remained in their normal lives. When your father mentioned going to the U.S. Marshals Service in Seattle, I didn't want to believe this was the reason, but it is."

"Why didn't you say something on the way here?" Frankie asked.

"In case I was wrong. It's a huge adjustment, and I didn't want you to start making it needlessly. But given Winnie's presence, I was right."

"That's correct. I work for the witness security division," Winnie chimed in. "I'm a caseworker who helps relocate the people in our protection. It will be my job to find you a new place to live, and a new identity. You will disappear as though Francesca Stiles never existed, and as though Francesca Paparella disappeared twenty-five years ago."

"Who?"

Kaden rubbed her hand. "You, Frankie. You were born Francesca Paparella. When you and your father went into the Witness Security Program, you became Francesca Stiles, and your father became Chris Stiles. And now you will become someone else and live somewhere else."

"No," Frankie whispered. "I want to go back to Nighthawk Farm. I want to go home. Does this mean I can never do that? What about the animals?" Her questions hung in the car with no response.

As the driver brought them to whatever "the facility" was, Frankie came to the realization that life as she knew it was over. But what did that mean?

"What's going to happen to my farm?"

"Eventually, the government will probably sell it. But as of this moment, Nighthawk Farm never existed," Winnie answered.

"Of course it did. I spent my whole life living and working on it, caring for it, and preparing myself to run it. It's everything to me." She bit her lip, trying not to cry.

Kaden gently squeezed her hand.

"Francesca," Winnie said gently. "If you want to stay alive, you have to forget everything about Nighthawk Farm and everything about Francesca Stiles. If someone in the future ever asks you about your farm, your answer must be, 'What farm?'"

Francesca swallowed, her heartbeat so loud she was certain the sound filled the car.

Winnie continued. "One slip could mean you're discovered, which in this case is a matter of life and death."

11

*W*hen the car reached a brick building, the driver pulled into a private parking garage filled with other cars like the one they were in. Winnie led them through a set of metal doors without saying a word.

Kaden walked down a long, dark hallway with Frankie beside him and worried for her future. *What will come of her? And what is this place?* Whatever the facility's purpose, it was kept locked and secure.

"Where is my father?" Frankie asked. "I thought he was going to be brought here."

Winnie replied, "He was taken to the hospital, but don't worry. He's under strict protective detail. As soon as he's released, he will join you here."

"Will that be today? What if the hospital keeps him for days?"

Winnie gave her a tight smile. "Then you'll be here for days. The accommodations are simple but secure." She typed a code on a panel by a heavy metal door and used her fingerprint to unlock it. The door clicked open, and she led the way down another dark hallway.

The heels of their shoes clicked along a shiny linoleum corridor, with metal doors along one side of the hall. Winnie stopped at the fifth door and put in another code along with her fingerprint. The door clicked, and she pulled it open to reveal an apartment inside.

"As I said, the living quarters are simple, but you will find everything you need, including a stocked pantry and refrigerator. Welcome to your home away from your future home. For now."

Frankie took a tentative step inside and stared back at him. "Are you coming?" Her voice trembled with fear.

Somehow, Kaden sensed that as soon as the door closed behind them, they wouldn't be getting out.

"Please, Kaden. Don't leave me alone." Frankie apparently understood she would be locked inside as well.

Winnie said, "There are two bedrooms, and there are cameras everywhere. You will be safe and have nothing to fear. It's not a prison." She ushered them inside.

Kaden stepped past Frankie and entered into a breakfast nook that led into a galley kitchen. As Frankie joined him and began opening the cabinets, he could see they contained dinnerware for four people. Everything was white and sterile. He moved toward the living room and brushed his fingers over a couch with vinyl upholstery. A television hung on the wall, with two windows on each side. Drapes were drawn so only a sliver of light filtered in from the edges. He stepped closer and lifted the edge of one of the drapes and froze.

It wasn't light that he'd seen, at least not sunlight. A brick wall was on the other side of the window, and the light was artificial, to give the illusion of a normal outdoor view.

He never believed himself to be claustrophobic, but his breath caught, and he struggled to fill his lungs.

"How long do you think we'll be in here?" he asked.

Winnie folded her arms across her chest, pulling the sleeves of her suit coat tight. "For Francesca, that will all depend on how quickly she can learn her new identity. You, on the other hand, are free to go whenever you wish."

"No," Francesca said. "Not yet. Please."

"Where will you send me?" He didn't want to upset Frankie, but he needed to know the plans they had for him. He had gotten such a small taste of freedom before suddenly someone else was calling the shots on his life again.

"You may tell us some places that you would like to go, and we will do our best to accommodate your preferences."

"I was already in the process of moving when a drone took my plane down. I'm going to Alaska, and no one is going to stop me. I have a life waiting for me there." And he wasn't about to give it up after he'd fought so hard for it.

"That is your right. You are not required to accept our help at all. But I do have to warn you that the Cordero family may hunt you down and kill you. You should take precautions."

"Cordero family? Who are they? And what do they have to do with Frankie?"

Frankie swayed on her feet, and he rushed to her to help her sit in one of the vinyl living room chairs.

"The Cordero family is an organized crime family out of Boston. They have been around for generations, and they are vicious. Daniel Paparella married into the Cordero family."

"Daniel?" Frankie said in a whimper. "Is that my father? Daniel Paparella?"

"Not anymore. And he can no longer live under the name Chris Stiles either. He will be given a new name like you."

"Was my mother's name Vera?"

"Your mother's name *is* Vera. Vera Cordero. She never received a new name because she refused to enter the program. She chose her family over her husband."

"And child," Frankie whispered.

Kaden's heart twisted in his chest at the pain on Frankie's face. It was one thing to learn her mother was still alive. It was a whole other to learn her mother had rejected her.

"She wants me dead," Frankie said. "Does she know we're being hunted down?"

"Yes, she would. I can't attest to her reasons for allowing it, but I'm sure she wasn't happy about how things worked out. The original caseworker for this situation died this past year. I took over the Cordero case after that. Your father provided the evidence law enforcement needed to put Cameron Cordero away for twenty-five years. Cordero was recently released from prison, but I wasn't notified. If I had been, I would've made sure your father was made aware as well."

"I don't understand. Why would my father have evidence against this man?"

Kaden wanted to embrace Frankie to comfort her. The information she was about to receive would crush her. He found her innocence refreshing, and after this, it would be gone.

"Frankie," he said, wanting to soften the blow by making sure it came from a friend. "The only way your father would have evidence like that would be if he was one of them." Winnie nodded confirmation, and he continued. "Daniel Paparella was part of the mob."

"Did you sleep okay?" Kaden's question sounded muffled to Frankie, and she squinted at him in confusion.

Two days had passed in a daze, and she didn't think she'd slept more than a few hours total in that time.

"Maybe I should ask if you slept at all." He chuckled as he went to sit beside her. He cringed at the sound of the plastic beneath them and wrapped an arm around her shoulders.

"I tried, but I hate this place." Her voice was groggy with defeat.

"It's temporary."

She longed to believe him, but without an actual end date, her stay in the facility felt interminable.

"Have you decided when you're leaving?" She held her breath as she waited for his answer.

"Yes. I'm going to Alaska today. I have to. I can't let anyone stop me. I haven't yet, and I'm not going to start now."

Frankie pulled back to face him, mere inches away. "I'm sorry you got involved in this mess."

"Don't be sorry. It's not your fault."

"But your life now is at risk because of me," she said.

"My life is better because of you."

She squinted again. "How?"

He removed his arm from around her and leaned forward on the couch, resting his elbows on his knees. "I've never met anyone like you. I come from a dog-eat-dog world of striving to be better than everyone, no matter the cost or sacrifice. When I left Boise, I was running away from it all. But then there you were in the middle of nowhere, showing me what being your own person is like."

"But I'm not my own person," Frankie protested. "I don't even know who I am."

"You're the same person you were yesterday and the day before that. They may change your name, but they can't change you. Don't let them, Frankie. You have to fight it."

Kaden shifted to face her, taking her hands in his. The intensity in his eyes suggested there was more at stake than a name change.

"What do you mean?" she whispered.

"You're different. You're not jaded by the way the world really works, and that's what makes you beautiful in this innocent, yet wild way." He reached a hand to her cheek. "You're what I imagine when I think of Alaska. It's why I've been drawn to the place. Why I've been drawn to you."

"Some might call me naive. Stupid, even. That was how I felt in community college."

He scoffed. "They would be wrong. They're looking at you with the eyes of the world. What society tells them is important. I left that way of thinking behind. There is more to this life than that, and you have it."

"I had it."

"*I* am sorry this is happening to *you*." His gaze fastened onto her lips. She knew he wanted to kiss her but wouldn't. The message he'd offered wasn't one of romance, but of comfort. But her heart wanted more.

"Kiss me," she whispered.

She didn't know if she would ever see him again. She didn't know if she would live another day. She was being hunted down like a wild animal after simply living her life and minding her own business. Nothing was certain in the world.

Tears filled her eyes at all she was losing due to factors outside her control. Including the man in front of her.

Kaden bent forward as Frankie met him halfway. Their lips touched gently, bringing the comfort she sought.

Kaden broke their connection and pressed his forehead to hers. When she opened her eyes, she saw he too had tears on his cheeks.

"It's not fair," she said. "I just met you."

He smiled through glistening eyes. "I won't tell you that life is fair because that would be a lie. But no matter where you go or what you do, I want you to go on believing anything is possible. Will you do that, for me?"

"Anything is possible?" She smiled. "Like maybe our paths will cross again?"

He chuckled. "I would like that very much. Anything is possible." He cupped her cheek again. "I'll hope for that too."

A knock on the door startled them, and they stood together as the door buzzed and opened.

Her father entered with Winnie, his arm in a sling and his back hunched in obvious remorse. Frankie couldn't let him think that she hated him. She had questions and concerns, but she loved her father despite his mistakes and flaws. There was no doubt in her mind that he loved her and had always done his best for her.

She went around the couch and wrapped her arms around him, careful not to touch his injured shoulder. "Papa, I'm so glad to see you alive."

"Francesca, I'm so sorry." He sobbed against her shoulder. "I had hoped you would never have to know. I tried to give you a good, safe life."

"I know." She didn't want to imagine the life he'd fled to give her that safety. There would be time to discuss it later. The priority was finding out what was next for them.

Frankie released Papa and faced Winnie. "I'm ready to get out of here. No offense, but I hate this place. I can't breathe here. I hope wherever you plan on sending us, there's a lot of open space."

"I can arrange for a country setting like your last caseworker did with the farm." Winnie turned her attention to Kaden. "Have you made your decision?"

"I have," he said, watching Frankie. "I'm keeping with my plan and going to Alaska. I'll take my chances on my own."

"Very well. I can walk you out." To Frankie, she said, "When I return, we'll practice answering to your new names. Before I drop you off anywhere, I have to be sure you won't slip up if someone ever calls out your present name. You'll also get a new personal history that you'll need to know as if you actually lived out every minute of it. Things like where you went to school or worked. Mr. Phillips, come with me."

Kaden walked around the couch but slowed his steps when he reached Frankie.

So this is it. She scrambled for some reason, any reason, to stop time, to stop what was coming. She had the sensation of being dragged toward the underground waterfall again. But she knew nothing would stop her from going over.

Kaden held out his hand to her father. "Sir, I wish you well."

Papa hesitated at first but shook Kaden's hand with his good arm. "Same to you, Kaden. I'm sorry we met under these circumstances, but now you know why I wanted you to leave sooner rather than later. It was never personal. Keep yourself safe, son. Don't ever let your guard down. Trust me."

Kaden nodded once and moved his attention to Frankie. They already said their goodbyes, but there was still so much she wanted to say. Her mind refused to give her the words.

"Keep hoping," he said with a wink.

Frankie smiled but pressed her lips to control it. "I won't ever stop."

He leaned close and kissed her on the cheek. Her eyes drifted closed as she breathed deeply of his essence.

"You can do this," he whispered against her ear.

Maybe, but I'm not sure how without you.

He left her, and she kept her eyes closed and her back to the door, unmoving until she heard the door close and the lock click behind her.

Kaden Phillips left her life as suddenly as he'd come into it—but she would never be the same again.

Two hours later, Kaden found himself still waiting in the U.S. Marshals' main office for the person who would assist him in getting back to his plane. He sat in a chair beside a desk piled high with a crooked stack of files. Whoever he was waiting for probably had no time to help him. Kaden considered heading to the exit and taking his chances on his own.

Then he thought of Greg's dead body.

One step out onto Seattle's city streets could prove the end of him. He didn't doubt that Cameron Cordero had a group of fine marksmen on rooftops outside.

Kaden remained seated but leaned back to view the long hallway of offices. He pretended to stretch when a man in a suit passed from one room to another.

Winnie had brought him there and said someone named Gary Herman would help him from that point. She needed to return to Frankie and Chris to assign their new location and identities.

The idea of there not being a Frankie Stiles in the world felt criminal. But at least she would still be alive. Frankie would always be her strong, graceful self, regardless of the name on her newly issued birth certificate. It would be nearly impossible for him to find her again without knowing her new name, but he supposed that was the point.

"Excuse me?" Kaden called out. "Are any of you Gary Herman?"

A man poked his head out of an office. "Gary doesn't work here anymore." His eyes narrowed as he exited the room and headed Kaden's way. "Is there something I can help you with?"

Kaden huffed with annoyance. "I guess Winnie didn't know about Gary's termination. She sent me in here to be processed out. I'm not entering the program."

"Is that so?" The man flipped through the files on the desk. "Which case is this for?"

"I don't have a number or anything, but it's Chris Stiles, or Daniel Paparella, or whatever you all refer to him as now."

"Interesting," the man murmured, riffling through each folder. "That file isn't here. She must have it."

"She?"

"Winnie," he confirmed. "This is her desk now. She was being trained to take over Gary's files after—well, he died last month. Car accident."

"Last month?" Kaden took in the mess on the desk. Had Winnie caused the disorganization, or were those files left over from Gary? "Was Gary the caseworker for Chris and Frankie Stiles?"

The other man nodded. "For twenty-five years."

"And Winnie took over his cases last month?"

"No, Winnie's still on probation. She hasn't been assigned any cases yet."

Kaden glanced back the way he had been let in by Winnie. "I'm confused. She's down there right now with Chris and Frankie, setting them up with new identities and homes. She told me Gary would help me get on my way. She seems to be handling their case on her own."

"What?" The man dropped the files and dashed back down the hall, banging on closed doors as he pulled a phone from his belt. "We may have identified our mole," he said into the phone. "Winnie Perkins.

Send security to the apartments immediately." To everyone peeking out of their offices, he gave the orders to get down to the apartments as well.

Kaden realized Winnie was not who she'd presented herself to be. She also had Frankie and Chris following her every order.

"Wait, what are you saying?" Kaden asked, following a few caseworkers out of the office space. His chest ached with pending doom, cutting oxygen off from reaching his lungs. "Is Winnie a threat?"

A team of agents and security guards burst into the hallway, guns at the ready.

Kaden didn't need any more information—he had his answer.

"Sir, for your safety, please remain here with the office staff while we handle this issue," a man dressed in a security uniform said, putting his hand on Kaden's chest to hold him back.

"I need to be there," Kaden said. "Frankie has to know she can't trust that woman."

"If she's there, we will tell her."

"*If?*" Adrenaline exploded through Kaden. He sidestepped the man and sprinted down the back stairs to catch up to the growing mass of workers descending on the apartment. The apartment door clicked open as Kaden wedged his way through the crowd. By the time he made it to the front, two men were exiting, their faces drawn and grim.

"They're gone," one of the men said, calling the police to have an APB put out on a black U.S. Marshals' vehicle, which may or may not have been used by an impostor going by the name of Winnie Perkins. For all any of them knew, Frankie and Chris could have been led out and shot in the streets, or taken far away to disappear forever.

A security guard approached the group. "They can't have gone far. The car left the facility minutes ago, eastbound."

Kaden forced his way back through the crowd and ran faster than he ever had in his life. Every footfall pained his lungs, but he wouldn't slow down. He reached an elevator but didn't have authorization to open it.

Banging on the gray metal, he shouted, "Somebody let me out!"

A burly guard approached from behind. "Sir, it's best if you go back to the office."

Kaden whirled on him. "I'm getting out of here if I have to take this place down brick by brick. You didn't vet your employee thoroughly enough when protecting people is your entire job, and now Frankie is gone and in more danger than she's ever been. If she dies, it's your fault."

The guard pinched his lips. "Get back to the office now. We can't do our job if we have to look out for you on top of everything else."

Kaden recognized that he wouldn't anywhere with the guard. He turned as if to go back to the office but didn't plan for a second on giving up so easily. He slunk through the group of agents who seemed busy planning their next move. When he reached the back of the group, he stayed low and waited for them to disperse. As they moved out, he slipped after them and took the set of stairs back up with them. When Kaden saw an exit door, he took it, stepping out into an alley.

In the next second, the door sealed with a definitive *thud* behind him. There was no going back. He peered toward the tops of the buildings around him, checking for armed guards.

Staying close to the side of the building, Kaden made his way toward the street. The guard had said Winnie had gone east. When he left the alley, he did the same, taking off at a run. If someone was going to take a shot at him, he wouldn't make it easy for them.

Two blocks down, he watched a U.S. Marshals' car fly by. Then he noticed a black car going north.

Frankie.

Kaden ran across the street to chase the car down, but it was going too fast.

"Taxi," he yelled with his hand raised. When a car pulled up, he jumped into the backseat. "Follow that black car. Hurry!"

Frankie sat beside her father in the same car that had transported her and Kaden to the facility days before. The differences were that Kaden wasn't here and Winnie had replaced the initial driver. Winnie had said it was for their safety, that the fewer people who knew their destination, the safer they would be. But since they'd left the facility, Winnie had shown a nervous edge that she didn't have before. Frankie lost track of the number of times the woman checked the rearview mirror. Frankie began twisting around in her seat to see for herself.

Did Winnie fear they were being followed by Cordero's men?

"Are you sure it was wise to come alone?" Frankie asked. "Isn't it risky if they realize we're in this car?"

"I'll get you there safely. I promise. Once we get out of this traffic."

Frankie glanced out the rear window and noticed a taxi weaving in and out of traffic. "Do the cab drivers in this city always drive so recklessly?"

"They're aggressive, but not usually at that level. But I'm sure that cab driver is just in a hurry. Don't worry. Nothing will stop me from completing this mission."

"What happened to Gary?" Papa asked. "He checked in with me not too long ago. Maybe about a month?"

"No, Papa," Frankie said gently. "Winnie said he passed away this past year. You must be mistaken."

"I am not. I may be getting old, but I still have all my faculties."

Winnie gave a short, brittle laugh. "Yes, it was about a month ago.

I'm sorry if I misled you, Francesca." She checked the mirror again.

Frankie contemplated how Winnie could have made such a mistake regarding a coworker's death. She didn't want to make anything of it, but it felt off somehow. In Winnie's line of work, Frankie imagined every detail mattered. The oversight painted Winnie as absent-minded, which seemed risky in her profession.

"Can you tell me anything about my mother?" Frankie asked. "Other than that she's alive and living in Boston?"

"I'm afraid I don't have many details to offer. She runs the Cordero family business, keeping their books," her father said.

"Was everything you told me about her true?" Frankie demanded. "Did you make any of it up?"

"Everything I said about her was true," Papa answered solemnly.

"Other than her death out on the lake. That memorial makes sense now. I wondered why you put a vow on it."

Her father broke their eye contact and transferred his gaze out his own window. "I kept you safe, but that didn't mean I stopped loving her. It broke my heart to leave her."

Frankie glimpsed a whole new side of her father, and it confused her even more. "What did you do for the Cordero family? How were you involved?"

"They were in the business of construction. On paper at least. After I got out of the marines, I went to work for them as a foreman."

"You were in the marines? I didn't know that."

Papa studied his hands, twisting them in his lap. "When I was assigned a new identity, my military history wasn't part of it. I had to forget it ever existed. But what I never forgot was how much I loved growing up on a farm. When you and I went into witness protection, I asked for secluded land in the mountains, and I got it. I don't regret anything."

"Not even leaving my mother behind?"

"Francesca, I gave her an opportunity to come with me. I begged her. She refused."

"Did she know you were taking me with you?"

He glanced back out the window and let silence fall between them in lieu of an answer.

"She was my mother," Frankie protested.

Papa stared at her. "I couldn't let you grow up in that monstrous family. You don't know what they're like, Francesca. They would have destroyed you."

"I saw what they did to Greg. He was killed in cold blood. I think I have an idea of what they're like."

"I'm so sorry," her father said softly. "I tried so hard to keep you away from all of that. Don't think for a second that I never missed my wife. I knew what kind of family she came from. But I fell in love with her, head over heels in love. I thought my love for her would steer her away from her family. She had a brilliant mind like you. She kept the books for her family's business. When she became pregnant, she was so ill that I took over for her. That's when I noticed a discrepancy in the bookkeeping and brought it to her attention. But instead of explaining, she told me to forget what I saw."

"And you didn't."

Papa scoffed, shaking his head. "Actually, I did. I cared too much about her and she was already so ill because of the pregnancy. So I let it go. But one night right after you were born, the feds showed up to grill me about a certain payment on the books. I did some digging and found out that the fee was for a hit ordered by Cameron, Vera's brother. Because I knew about the order, and because Vera knew, we could have been sent to prison. So I cut a deal. We would go into witness protection if I agreed to give evidence. When Vera refused,

I said I wouldn't do it unless they gave her immunity. The feds agreed, and Cameron went to prison alone."

"Until recently," Francesca whispered.

Papa glared at Winnie. "We should have been informed that Cameron was released."

"I've apologized for that already," Winnie said, her tone even and cold. "I came on staff to fill Gary's absence, and I hadn't gone through all of his files yet. And no one knew I was the new caseworker, so no one told me about Cameron's release. The timing was unfortunate."

"A bloodbath isn't merely unfortunate, especially when it could have been avoided altogether," Papa said.

Tension mounted inside the car, but Winnie didn't reply.

In the next second, Winnie screeched to a halt in the middle of an intersection as a black SUV cut them off at the front.

Winnie jumped from the front seat, gun drawn, and approached the SUV that had cut them off. But the vehicle backed up and surged toward her. Winnie flung herself out of the way but was able to shoot at the driver as the SUV passed her by. Her bullets missed, and the SUV raced toward the car that held Frankie and her father. It came to a stop in front of Frankie's door, and she heard her father inhale sharply.

"Vera!" he cried out.

The taxi that had been following them aggressively stopped behind them, and Kaden jumped out of the back seat. He ran straight for Frankie and yanked open her door. "Come on. You can't stay in there."

She grabbed her backpack, but when she glanced back at her father, he had yet to take his eyes off the woman driving the SUV.

"I believe that's my mother," she said to Kaden.

"Get in," Vera said. She craned her head around to see Winnie storming toward them, her gun drawn—and aimed right at Frankie. "She will kill you if you don't come with me. Get in *now*."

"Winnie, what are you doing?" Frankie cried.

Frankie sought out her father for guidance, but the man was already dashing toward Vera's SUV as if a rope pulled him toward his wife. He launched himself into the passenger seat and stared at the woman.

"We have no choice. Winnie will kill us," Kaden said as he knelt behind the opened rear door. He used it as protection against Winnie's bullets. "Winnie's a plant hired by the Cordero family to kill you. She probably killed Gary."

"But my mother keeps the Corderos' books. How is that any safer?" Frankie demanded.

"Right now she's your only way out. We have to go." Kaden pulled her out of Winnie's car and into the rear seat of Vera's, pushing her flat against the upholstery.

Winnie's bullet fractured the rear window over their heads.

Vera stomped on the gas, and the SUV took off down the next street where no more bullets could hit them.

Kaden straightened enough to shut the door, then wrapped his arms around Frankie. She clung to him in terror and uncertainty.

Had they made the right choice in trusting Vera?

No one said anything for a long time, and Frankie kept her head down until she couldn't any longer. Her mother was behind the wheel, and Frankie had to see her.

For the first time in her life, she glimpsed the profile of the woman who'd given birth to her. Vera, an elegant woman with her brown hair pulled up in a perfect twist, had been dead to her for her whole life but was somehow sitting less than three feet away, alive and well. But Frankie knew nothing about the woman or her plans for them.

"Do you mean to keep us safe, or do you mean to kill us?" Frankie asked point blank.

Vera answered without missing a beat. "I will do what's best for my family, as I always have. Do as I say, and you have a good chance of staying alive."

It wasn't an answer that brought comfort. Frankie leaned against Kaden's shoulder, realizing they had gone from the clutches of one killer to another.

13

The Seattle sights flashed by in a blur as Vera drove through the city. The Space Needle stood prominently against the backdrop of a towering Mount Rainier, and for all Kaden knew, Vera Cordero was taking them into the mountains to kill them herself. He watched Chris for direction, but the man hadn't said a word since he'd climbed into the front seat. Would he allow Vera to kill their daughter after all he had done to protect her? Would Vera kill Chris for taking her daughter from her? Judging by the woman's coldness toward them all, she'd built up twenty-five years' worth of resentment.

Kaden had so many questions, but who was he to ask them? He was nothing to Frankie, nothing more than a stranger who had been in the wrong place at the wrong time.

Except, as he held her close and felt the fear in her tense muscles, he questioned if he had been exactly where he was supposed to be at the perfect time. Everything would have still happened the way it had, whether he had been by her side or not. The idea of her facing all of it alone made him sick to his stomach. She would have been shot if he hadn't pushed her down in her kitchen to shield her from bullets. Without his plane, she would have been killed.

He tightened his hold on her, and she lifted her face to him. The anguish in her eyes undid him.

"You should have stayed away," she whispered. "If you die now, it'll be my fault."

"I'm right where I'm supposed to be." And he was. Kaden didn't belong anywhere else but holding Frankie and making sure she stayed alive. "Why don't you try to get some sleep? I'll keep watch and wake you if anything changes."

Her fingers gripped the front of his shirt as she shook her head. "I couldn't sleep a wink. Thank you for coming back."

"As soon as I realized Winnie was corrupt, nothing was going to stop me from finding you. I saw her car and grabbed a cab to keep up with you."

Frankie's lips curled into a smile. "She knew it too. You made her so nervous."

"We're going to get out of this," he assured her.

She glanced at the back of her father's head.

"I feel so betrayed by Papa," she whispered. "He would have left me behind back there. I don't even know him anymore." She gazed toward her mother with a lifetime of longing in her eyes. Frankie was feeling betrayed by her father and rejected by her mother. Kaden wished he could command both of the adults to grow up. Couldn't they see how they were hurting their daughter?

Kaden examined Chris's profile. The old man was so forlorn. Had he given up so easily the moment he saw his wife? It was as if Chris knew he'd lost the battle, and he knew there was no other choice but to return to the life he'd fled.

"She deserves an explanation from both of you," Kaden said, unable to keep the anger from his voice. How was he, a stranger who'd known Frankie less than a week, the one who was prioritizing her care rather than her own parents?

Frankie touched his arm with a shake of her head. She may not want him to speak up, but he couldn't sit there and pretend everything was fine. The situation was anything but the happy family reunion Frankie deserved.

To his surprise, Vera answered him. "You're right, Kaden. I commend you for standing by Francesca. There aren't many people who would be as brave as you. I can think of another person in this car who turned tail and ran."

"I could say the same," Chris snapped, "except you ran to your daddy."

"Enough!" Frankie shouted.

Kaden put his hand on her forearm, but not to stop her from speaking. He wanted her to know he was there for her.

She squeezed his hand and continued. "I would say I don't recognize either of you, but the truth is I never really knew either of you to begin with. My whole life has been a lie and everything I thought to be true isn't." Frankie kept her attention on Vera as she spoke. "I was told you were dead. But you're not. You've been alive this whole time. Did you ever think to search for me? Or did nothing else matter as long as you made your family happy?"

Vera didn't reply.

"That's what I thought," Frankie said. "You have no place to criticize Papa when you didn't come after me."

"Exactly," Chris said smugly.

Frankie cut him off. "Don't act sanctimonious, Papa. You had twenty-five years to tell me the truth. You told me my mother drowned in the lake. I've been afraid to go out there my whole life. Your lies kept me paralyzed with fear."

"Better afraid than dead," Chris said.

"I disagree, Papa. Better prepared than dead. Your lies nearly got me killed because I had no idea what was going on. I could still die today, all because you kept me in the dark. How can I trust you now? And why should I trust you, *Vera*? You abandoned me."

"You're still not going anywhere," Vera replied evenly. "You might as well get comfortable. We have a long ride ahead of us."

"Where are you taking us?" Frankie demanded.

Vera refused to answer, and her tense jaw made it clear she wouldn't be offering any more details. Kaden pulled Frankie close and as the ride stretched into hours, Frankie drifted to sleep on his shoulder.

Kaden didn't dare close his eyes. He wanted to know their exact location the whole time. When he saw signs for Idaho, he wondered if Vera planned to drive them across the country.

At the next gas station stop, Frankie stirred, and as he led her to the restrooms, he told her his plan. "I'm going to get us to Boise."

"To your parents' house? Are you sure about that?" Her brow furrowed in confusion.

He felt the same way, but under the circumstances, going home seemed like the safest option. "I'm not exactly excited about it, but it's the best plan we've got."

"All you wanted was to be free in Alaska. I am so sorry." She touched his arm. "Now you've lost your freedom again."

He reached for her hand. "I don't want to hear any more apologies. All I want is for you to be safe. I want you to have your life back. And when you do, I'll be free to be free." He pulled her in for a hug and tried to absorb her belief in him. He would need it to make his plan work.

When they returned to the car, Vera and Chris were talking low. Kaden couldn't make out their conversation, but the tension spoke volumes. Neither was smiling, but twenty-five years of separation surely built animosity.

"I'd like to ask if you would be willing to let me go when we get to Boise," Kaden said, not caring that he was interrupting the conversation. "I have nothing to do with this family feud, and I don't want to be involved. I don't want to know anything about your business or your past. I have my own family to deal with."

Vera watched him, and he could see her calculating the possible outcomes of his request.

Kaden held his breath, trying to act nonchalant and callous. Any fear on his face might encourage Vera to get rid of him permanently. If he posed a threat against her and her family in any way, he had no doubt she would kill him. "I'm sure having me along is messing with your plans to fix your family."

Vera glanced in Chris's direction and then appraised Frankie. "What would make you happy?" she asked her daughter.

Frankie blanched in indecision. She sought out Kaden for his input, but he couldn't give it verbally. He shrugged to show he didn't care one way or the other and prayed she would pick up on his cue to behave the same. If she showed she cared in any way, Vera would stop his plan to break free.

"What would make me happy is if you sent me and Kaden to Alaska," Frankie finally said. "You wouldn't ever have to hear from us again. I don't know anything about you, your family, or your business, so I'm not a threat to you. At least Papa's lies were good for something."

"No," Chris said sternly. "You will stay with me, where I can keep an eye on you. Kaden can go, but you will stay."

"Interesting," Vera said, eyeing her estranged husband. "My father once told me the same thing, and I lost my child because I listened. Tell me, Daniel, why shouldn't I make you lose her now?"

"Vera, you had your chance—"

"Stop. I'm not interested in your excuses." Vera aimed a lethal gaze at them all. "Everyone, get back in the car. Boise it is. But we're all staying together."

Kaden's affluent Boise suburb was beyond Frankie's imagination. Every house they passed was more exorbitant than the last, from stately brick structures to floor-to-ceiling glass walls. And those were only the homes she could see from the road. Many were shielded behind gates and full, mature trees.

"It's the next place on the left," Kaden told Vera. "You can't see the actual house, but it's the one with the ostentatious cherubs on the top of the gateposts."

Frankie giggled, then sobered when the driveway came into view. "Oh, you were serious."

"Unfortunately." He winked at her.

Vera pulled into the driveway and stopped at the black box that required a code. "What is it?"

Kaden laughed. "There is no way I'm telling you the security code to my family's estate."

Vera gave him a sickeningly sweet smile in the rearview mirror. "Since we will all be your very special guests, you might as well tell me now."

He snorted. "You're joking."

"I told you we would all be staying together. This place seems secure enough. Now give me the code."

The glare Kaden sent at the back of Vera's head made Frankie's stomach churn. She feared for his safety within the walls of his own home. Vera was a stranger, relation or not. She hadn't honored her marriage vows and had chosen to stay with her criminal family. Frankie had no reason to trust her, and Kaden definitely shouldn't.

Frankie also recalled Vera's words from earlier. She planned to make Papa pay by taking his child away from him, as he had done to her. With Vera running things, they were all at her whim.

Frankie squeezed Kaden's hand, in a silent urge to comply.

"Fine." He issued a series of numbers.

Vera punched in the code, then waited for the gates to open. But nothing happened.

"Are you sure that's it?" Vera asked.

"Of course I'm sure. You must have punched it in wrong. Try it again."

Vera punched the code again, slowly and for all to see. Still, nothing happened. "Apparently you've been locked out. Problems at home?"

Kaden mumbled under his breath in confusion, then said, "Let me out."

Vera unlocked the rear doors, and he climbed out to go to the gate. Gripping the bars, he peered between them. Frankie wondered what he was searching for. When he returned to the car, he tried the code himself. When it still didn't work, he hit the intercom button.

A voice carried through the speaker. "How can I help you?"

"Jared, it's Kaden. My code's not working. Did it get changed?"

"Yes, your father ordered a new code, and I'm sorry, but I'm not to share it."

"Not even with me?" Kaden asked. "What's going on?"

"I will ask if I can let you in, Mr. Kaden," Jared said in an apologetic tone.

"Ask? That's ridiculous. This is my house."

No response came, and Frankie figured the gatekeeper was making the call to ask Mr. Phillips. She felt bad for Kaden, who must feel rejected and embarrassed, not to mention as frightened as she was of Vera's wrath.

"Kaden, we can go someplace else," Frankie said, leaning out the window to speak quietly to him. "We don't have to stay here, even if we're allowed to."

"You better hope they let us in," Vera warned.

Frankie eyed her mother's stare in the mirror. What would Vera do if they were turned away from the mansion?

"Leave him alone," she told her mother. "You chose to keep him with us. You could have set him free, and you still could. Leave us. Drive away right now and never look back, and make everyone happy."

"Don't talk to your mother like that." Papa's reprimand stunned Frankie, but before she could tell him she didn't see Vera as her mother and never would, the gates swung open.

"Get back inside," Vera instructed Kaden, and he followed her order.

Frankie shifted back to her side to make room, but he took her hand to keep her close. His hand was clammy. He was nervous, but from what? Her mother's intentions, or his father's?

Frankie braced herself to meet his parents, knowing it wouldn't be a warm welcome. There would be no celebratory feast brought in for the reception. They might not even get out of the car.

"When we arrive, you are to introduce us as Francesca Cordero and her parents, Vera and Daniel Cordero. Don't try anything heroic." Vera glared in the mirror at them. "Do you understand?"

"Yes, but they won't care who you are. Not unless you whip out your bank account records."

"That can be arranged," Vera replied smugly.

So far, Frankie was not impressed with the woman. She wished she'd never met her, but she was also glad that she could finally let go of the fantasy that her childhood mind had dreamed up about her mother. Vera didn't fit the maternal figure Frankie had always imagined. The woman most likely carried multiple guns and a knife, not including her sharp tongue.

Vera drove the car through a winding drive, lush with greenery on all sides. Finally, an expansive white marble home with stately columns appeared behind a circular driveway. A limousine was parked under a porte cochere with more white columns.

"It's like something out of the Greek mythology books I read when I was a kid," Frankie said.

"Well, the people inside think of themselves as gods, so that matches up." Kaden's demeanor worried Frankie.

She glanced at her mother and muttered, "Seems to be going around."

A man in a black suit and white shirt stepped from the house and down four marble stairs. He opened the rear door. "Mr. Kaden, welcome back."

"'Back'? Not 'home'? What's going on, Jared? Why was my code changed?"

"I'm not at liberty to say. Your father is waiting for you in his office. Your mother has taken to her room."

"Figures." Kaden climbed from the car. "Might as well get this over with. Jared, this is the family that helped me after my plane went down. They'll be staying tonight. Can you arrange for three rooms?"

"Certainly. I'm sure Mr. Phillips will want to thank them formally as well. I will park the car in the garage."

Frankie watched her mother's reaction to giving the car over to the hired help, but if Vera was concerned about it, she didn't let on. She left the car running and climbed out. She took in the building from corner to corner, and then she eyed the trees.

"This will be fine," she said under her breath. To Jared, she said, "Will the gate remain locked at all times?"

"Yes ma'am."

She smiled at Jared. "You are obviously a commendable steward. I'm sure you would never allow any riffraff inside, no matter what sob story they gave you. Am I correct?"

Jared cleared his throat and kept his gaze above her head. "Never."

Vera exuded elegance and an obvious wealthy upbringing as she patted his shoulder. "Good man."

Jared said, "I will show you to your rooms. Mr. Kaden, please see your father right away."

As Kaden ran up the steps and disappeared behind wooden doors with intricate glass inserts, Frankie fell in step with Vera and Papa. Her mother fit perfectly with the opulent house, but Frankie and Papa looked like they should be shown the gardener's quarters out back. Fortunately, if Jared thought so, he didn't show it.

They entered the home, and Frankie inhaled sharply. Papa coughed once and covered his mouth. Vera followed Jared up the large marble steps in the center of the two-story foyer as if she were entering her own home. If Frankie had thought she and Vera had something in common because they both had overbearing fathers who'd kept them from leaving home, the similarities ended there. In fact, Frankie wondered if her mother hadn't left her family because she knew she could never live in an old ranch house on a farm.

Frankie took the stairs, trying to release more of that childhood fantasy about her mother. The two of them were night and day. Frankie slowed her steps and let the physical gap between them lengthen, though she doubted it would ever match the emotional chasm between them. She needed to remember that Vera Cordero wasn't merely different.

She was dangerous.

14

"*W*hy was my code changed?" Kaden demanded as he entered his father's office.

Malcolm Phillips sat behind a mahogany desk, signing a piece of paper. His perfectly combed black hair appeared grayer in the desk's lamplight than the last time Kaden had seen him.

Has it really been a week? It felt like so much longer.

Bookshelves filled with leather-bound law volumes adorned in gold leaf numbers surrounded them on three sides. Kaden knew not a single one had ever been opened.

"I thought you said you were moving to Alaska," his father replied without raising his head.

"I was. I *am*. But that doesn't mean I should be locked out of this place. It's still my home."

"You can't have it both ways. You took your money and bought a plane. Where is that plane now?" He signed with a flourish of his expensive fountain pen, then dropped it on the desk.

"At the Seattle airport," Kaden said, though he couldn't be sure. "I plan to have it inspected by a professional before I take it to Alaska." He crossed his arms over his chest. "I find changing the gate code childish and beneath you."

His father rubbed his clean-shaven face and leaned back in his burgundy leather chair. He wore a perfectly pressed white shirt and tan slacks. "Shall we discuss all the childish things *you* have done of late? Spending your trust fund on a plane is one of many."

Kaden couldn't let the conversation get away from him. "My plane is not a toy. It's an investment in my future and career."

"Your career was to act as counsel for this family. Your education was *my* investment into the family business and your future marriage."

"And that's the real reason the code was changed. Admit it. You're still upset that I didn't marry Julia, so you changed the code. Like I said, childish."

His father stood abruptly, leaning over his desk with his fingers spread across the top. "I changed the code because this is my home. You made your choice, and I'm honoring it. This is not your home any longer. You have a lot of nerve coming back here after you discarded everything your mother and I have done for you."

"You mean for yourself."

Malcolm balled his hands into fists and slammed them on the desk. His face grew red as he said in a barely controlled voice, "I will not be subjected to your insolence. While you are under my roof, you will do as I say. Or you can leave right now, and the next time, the gate won't be opened to you."

Kaden felt himself spinning toward the door to do just that. As he had done the last time he and his father had the very same discussion. Somehow he was back where he'd started, with the same decision to make. Stay or leave. Live under Malcolm Phillips's iron fist or find his own way in the wilds of Alaska.

What had changed was that if he stormed out of his father's office again, it could mean being gunned down in the street. And not only him, but Frankie and Chris as well. Vera might be safe. For all he knew, she was another plant like Winnie, sent to lure them to a certain place for the slaughter. Or to kill them herself. Either way, he couldn't go anywhere. He wouldn't be another person in Frankie's life who endangered her for his own selfish reasons.

He swallowed hard. "I'll play by your rules—for now. I brought back the family who has been helping me with my plane. Jared is readying their rooms. I landed on their back property in Washington. I wouldn't be alive without them."

Although you probably wish they hadn't been there to help me because if I won't obey you like a good little boy, you'd like nothing better than to see me fail.

He held back that thought and continued. "I'm going to ask you to be kind to my guests. Your quarrel is with me, not with them."

"Who are they? I'll need to do a background check before I allow any of them to stay overnight. I will not be robbed blind by strangers."

"Right, we can't have anyone stealing the gaudy busts all over this museum. What else will we use to give our guests nightmares? As if our personalities aren't enough."

"Name." Malcolm readied his pen, ignoring Kaden's dig.

"Stiles—no, wait." Kaden remembered what Vera had instructed him to say. He didn't understand why she would want her corrupt family's name to be used. It was a sure way to get his father to call the cops on them. But that might be a good thing. "Cordero. Daniel and Vera Cordero, and their daughter, Francesca."

His father wrote out the names. "You're dismissed."

It was how every conversation between them ended. No matter what was said during the discourse, his father would always put him back in his place with those two simple words. They reminded Kaden who would always have the final say in their dysfunctional relationship. The one time Kaden had bested him was the day he'd flown out. And boy, had it felt good.

Too bad the victory had been short-lived. If Kaden didn't know better, he might have thought his father sabotaged his plane to take him out. Malcolm had a hefty insurance policy on him. Perhaps even more than marrying into Julia's family would have given him.

His father raised his eyebrows. "Did you not hear me? I said you're dismissed."

Kaden felt like he was five years old again. His tongue felt thick in his mouth and saying what he really wanted to say was impossible.

Why can't you love me as I am, rather than on your terms? Why will I never be good enough for you?

"Please just be nice to my guests," Kaden said, and turned his back to leave.

"Dinner's at six. Dress appropriately."

Kaden fingered the open denim shirt and T-shirt which had been white before he left Idaho. So much had happened between then and the present, and the shirt showed the evidence of his survival. A loving father would want to hear every detail of his son's harrowing brushes with death, would want to know how he could help.

But Malcom Phillips loved only one thing—money.

The Phillipses' dining room was supposedly located at the back of the house, but Frankie and her father had yet to find it. They followed a long hallway with red carpet and portraits of people from past generations along the dark wood walls.

"I wonder who these people are," Frankie mused.

"No one of significance," Papa responded quickly.

"How do you know?" she asked, surprised. "I doubt the Phillips family would hang them if they weren't important."

Papa wrinkled his nose. "It's all pretense. The whole house smells of new money."

Frankie slowed her steps, intrigued by a new side of her father she had never known. Her whole life, he had been a simple farmer. She didn't think he'd graduated from high school. But that had all fabricated for his new identity. The U.S. Marshals Service had made it all up, and the real man her father had been—every success and failure—had been erased from existence. She studied his face, and she realized his whole demeanor had changed since she'd learned the truth.

"You walk straighter," she said.

"Pardon?"

She giggled. "You even talk differently. You've never said 'pardon' in my life."

"I'm the same person you've always known. I'm still your father."

"But who were you, Papa? Before?"

He opened another door, which opened to a home theater. "Ridiculous," he muttered. "It's like these people checked off all the boxes on what should be included to show off their wealth rather than what might actually serve in a functional home."

"You're changing the subject."

Papa glanced at the last set of doors. They must lead to the dining room and would be his escape from responding to her. She expected him to take the way out as he had so many times before.

But he met her gaze. "Francesca, I had an opportunity to start over. I didn't like who I was. Let Daniel Paparella go. I don't regret anything. I'm not him anymore. The one person I care about being is your father, no matter what our names are."

"I wasn't speaking about your time married to the mob. I was talking about who you were before that. Papa, you left your family too. I know nothing about them. Do I have grandparents? Aunts or uncles?"

"When I married your mother, my own family disowned me. They said I was making a huge mistake." He scoffed. "They were right."

"Did you graduate from high school?"

"And college."

"College and the marines? Wow. I have so many questions."

"Not today, Francesca. Today, we put on the facade that we come from money, or I don't doubt these people will give us the boot."

"Vera seems to have the act covered."

"Your mother isn't acting. She doesn't need to pretend."

"Stop calling her that. She's not my mother. We have nothing in common, and she has done nothing for me. For all I know, she'll kill me the first chance she gets."

The fact that Papa didn't deny her concerns told her he shared them.

He lowered his voice and said, "I made sure our rooms are connected. If she tries anything to harm you during the night, I will stop her."

"Why did you even get in her car? It was as if you were in a trance."

"I knew she was our only hope at that moment."

"But at what cost? All your work to break free from this family has now been for nothing. Papa, what will they do to you?"

"Don't worry about me, Francesca. I'm a survivor. But I promise you, I won't leave you. I promise you that you will get out of this alive, even if I have to go back to that life. I will do whatever it takes to keep you safe."

The image of her father living in corruption and crime made her physically ill. "I don't want you to go back to that life. I don't know much about it, but I do know you've sacrificed enough—no, too much—for me already."

Papa reached for her and wrapped her in a tight hug. He whispered in her ear, "You must do everything to stay alive. Whatever it takes. And trust no one."

"Not even Vera," she whispered back.

Papa stepped back with a frown. "I want to say you can trust her, but I don't know."

Frankie glanced at the doors, knowing Vera was already inside.

"Do you still love her, even after today?"

"Francesca, that's not—"

"Answer the question. You wrote *Until Death Do Us Part* on her memorial. You never remarried. Why?"

"I wasn't going to bring someone else into this family to be in danger with us. Plus, if Vera ever found out . . ." He whistled low at the thought.

"It sounds as if you fear her. But do you love her?"

The doors swung open, and someone who resembled Kaden stood with his hands on the doorknobs.

"There you are." His smile was identical to Kaden's.

But his clothes and hair were not.

Suddenly, Frankie realized she and her father were not dressed for the fancy meal. She wore her light-blue cotton overalls, the last clean pants she had left in her backpack, and a yellow-and-white checkered blouse.

"I feel like a country bumpkin. Maybe this isn't a good idea." She peered inside to see Vera and another woman in fine clothes chatting by a glowing fire. Both women wore black dresses. "This is definitely not a good idea. Tell them I was too tired to come to dinner."

As Frankie stepped backward, Kaden clasped his hand into hers and held tight. He pulled her close and kissed her cheek. "You are perfect as you are. Please stay with me. I need you for support," he whispered.

Frankie's eyes drifted closed. "The feeling's mutual."

He chuckled against her ear, causing a shiver to race up her spine.

A man clearing his throat from somewhere in the room made Kaden jump back, severing their connection. A cold shiver followed the pleasant one from Kaden as she caught a glimpse of the man who must be his father.

His gaze raked over her from head to toe. By the time he made it back up to her face, disdain covered his. "Vera, is this your help?"

Vera threw back her head and laughed. "Why, Malcolm, this is my daughter. She enjoys embarrassing me whenever she has the opportunity. Please excuse her attire this once. We'll be sure to address this later, won't we, Francesca?"

Frankie didn't know what else she could wear. All she had were jeans.

Her father nudged her elbow and reminded her they had to keep the charade going.

"Yes, Mother." She kept her head down. "I apologize, sir, for my poor taste in jokes."

"And wardrobe." To Vera, he said, "My son tries me as well. I understand your disappointment. Shall we sit down to eat?"

Frankie caught Kaden rolling his eyes at her. At least he had known to dress up. He approached her and offered her his arm, tugging her hand into the crook of his elbow when she didn't know what she should do. She couldn't afford to slip up again.

At the table, Kaden held out the chair next to her mother, pushing it in once Frankie was seated. Frankie saw her father do the same for Vera, then both men walked around the table to sit across from them. Mr. and Mrs. Phillips sat on the ends of the oval table, draping their napkins on their laps.

Frankie mimicked their every move, even sipping water from tall glasses. As she put the glass down, Kaden's face came into view above the rim, and he winked at her.

Stop, she mouthed.

He feigned innocence, but she needed him to understand they needed to stay under the radar, or they could be kicked out and become target practice to the men chasing them down.

"I must say how honored we are to have you in our home," Mrs. Phillips said to Vera and Papa.

"Thank you, Mrs. Phillips," Vera said.

"Call me Denise. I insist. You are our cherished guests for however long you need."

Frankie felt her eyes bulge before she could stop them.

Kaden's surprise was also written on his face, but he recovered faster than she did. "Thank you, Mother, for being so welcoming to this family who helped me in my time of need."

The woman's smile tightened on her face. "How lucky of you to land on such a prominent family's property."

"Prominent?" Frankie said, glancing at her father diagonally from her.

"Sweetheart," Vera said with that sickly sweet laugh again. "You're always full of jokes. Of course prominent. The Cordero family is known far and wide."

Mr. Phillips said, "When I did a little preparation to equip me with meaningful conversation tonight, I learned that your family line extended from Boston to Washington. Very impressive."

"Yes, we've branched out to buy more land," Vera said. "There's so much out west. And speaking of property, I took a walk through your gardens along the river. They're absolutely stunning. You have a prime location, Malcolm. Well done."

"Thank you, Vera. Your accolades mean a great deal. Perhaps I should seek out some land purchases as well. I'm looking for another venture to invest in. My most recent one fell through."

Malcolm narrowed his eyes at Kaden for a split second. It was fast, but Frankie didn't miss it, and neither did Kaden. She also noticed Kaden's shoulders had folded in a bit, and he fiddled with the soup the footman had placed before him. Frankie realized Kaden had begun to believe his parents might be grateful for the help he had received at Nighthawk Farm. But that wasn't the case. Malcolm and Denise were honored to have someone from the renowned Cordero family in their home. They believed such a visit would elevate their status.

How pretentious. Especially when what the Cordero family was renowned for was organized crime.

"We've been honored to have Kaden in our home at Nighthawk Farm, right, Father?" Frankie said, smiling at Kaden. She hoped to convey that she wasn't acting.

Kaden relaxed, and his eyes softened with appreciation. "Thank you, Francesca. That means the world to me. You mean the world to me."

A heavy silence fell on the table, but Frankie was oblivious to it until Malcolm broke it. "Denise, didn't you have a message for our son?"

"A message? Oh, a message, yes!" Denise clapped her hands once. "Kaden, Julia would like to speak with you. She's called here to inquire about you twice now. Please return her call promptly following dinner. Invite her over tomorrow, or even tonight. I think she's had a change of heart."

Kaden blanched. "Mother, that's not going to happen. Julia and I have said all we needed to each other. We're both content with the decision to call off the wedding."

Frankie dropped her gaze to her plate. She tried to stay out of the conversation, but the bite of chicken lodged in her throat. She reached for her water and caught Kaden's pleading expression. He was trying to assure her there was nothing between him and Julia.

Malcolm's voice hardened. "You will call her tonight. Do you understand?"

Kaden took his napkin and pressed it to his lips. His eyelids closed, and he nodded once.

Suddenly, Frankie felt her resolve to pretend to be some rich family evaporate. She didn't like the way Kaden's parents treated him and needed some fresh air to clean away the arrogant airs they put on.

"If you'll excuse me, I'm tired from our drive." She pushed back from the table as Kaden jumped up to help her. "I can move my own chair. I've been doing it my whole life. It really is a silly custom, and so degrading. Like being told who you'll marry in this day and age."

"Francesca," Vera interrupted, with an obvious warning in her voice. "You're obviously tired because you're not yourself tonight. You're excused. Go get some rest."

Frankie glanced around the table, but no one spoke up or lifted a finger to put a stop to the charade—not even Kaden.

Why is he going along with this?

With her attention locked on Kaden, she said, "At least I know where I stand with you all. Good night."

As she left the room, she could hear her mother apologizing for her yet again, and Malcolm saying, "You send your children to prestigious universities, and they return with crazy ideas about dreams and injustices. Eventually though, they come back around. They simply need a little persuasion. Isn't that right, Kaden?"

As the double doors closed behind her, she paused to await his response in the hope he would refuse his father's orders to resume his relationship with Julia. But all Kaden said was, "Yes, sir," and she knew she had been wrong about him.

Completely wrong.

15

*L*ater that night, a full moon lit the sky over the river, casting shadows along a private brick pathway that wove through the Phillips family property. Kaden walked slowly with his hands in the pockets of his dress pants, thinking about how he'd messed up at dinner.

I let her down like everyone else in her life.

Frankie's disappointment in him was well deserved, and he wouldn't blame her if she never spoke to him again.

"Regret is a horrible feeling," came a woman's deep voice from the shadows. "Trust me, I know."

Kaden paused and narrowed his gaze to make out the person hidden within a cloak of darkness. "Vera?" he asked cautiously. Had the woman followed him?

She stepped forward to show herself. "I was here first."

Her answer to his unspoken question surprised him.

"But I'm glad to see you out here," she continued. "It gives us a chance to talk."

"Do we have to?" he asked.

Her laugh was smooth and deep, so different than the high-pitched laugh she'd used at dinner. He liked it better. But he didn't want to like anything about the woman who held them captive.

"Let's walk." She moved forward.

He almost refused, but he'd already failed miserably that night. Might as well keep at it.

Their steps tapped in unison against the bricks—his loafers and her heels. "What do you want?" he asked.

"It's not what you think. I kept you with us because I saw Frankie's fondness for you."

Vera's use of the nickname caught him off guard. He hadn't heard Vera call her daughter "Frankie" before. The way she said it made him smile a bit too. It sounded like a term of endearment.

Kaden shook the thought away. The woman was dangerous. Nothing could endear her to him. "Frankie and I are friends."

"I see." They walked slowly for a few minutes, then Vera said, "Do you love this Julia woman?"

He stopped walking. "Not that it's any of your business, but let me be perfectly clear. Julia and I are friends, and nothing more."

He could practically feel Vera smile. "I knew it. You do like my Francesca."

Kaden rubbed his forehead, knowing he gave too much away. "This is why I was a horrible attorney," he grumbled, causing Vera to laugh that smooth rolling sound again. Surprisingly, it relaxed him.

"You're funny. I can see why Frankie likes you."

"Not anymore. After tonight, she knows what a coward I am. She's better off knowing now though. Before she thinks there could ever be something between us."

"Why can't there be?" Vera began walking again, her voice lulling him to stay with her.

"The Cordero name may work for dinner, but when the truth comes out that Frankie is a farmer, my father will send one of us away, or both, and not together."

"Do you always do what your father says?" Vera prodded.

"Don't you?"

She laughed. "Touché." After a pause, Vera asked, "What if there was a way the two of you could be together, and your parents would be satisfied enough to leave you alone?"

"That will never happen. I couldn't even manage to run away without having to come right back. My father's grip on me is too strong."

"You had to come back because of me, and for that I'm sorry. To be honest, I didn't know you existed when I came for my daughter. Had I known, I might have let you take her to Alaska. If the opportunity arises to go again, will you go?"

"I left my plane on the tarmac in Seattle. It has to be repaired correctly before I can use it to transport people. My father will not give me more money, not when he reminds me every day how much I owe him for law school. No, Alaska is done."

"That's sad."

"Why are you asking me this?" It felt wrong to share his private thoughts with such a woman. Would she use anything he said against him?

Vera dodged the question. "What did you think of Frankie's response to the idea of you calling Julia?"

Kaden shrugged. "I thought she was braver than me."

"I see. Well, you have a good night, Kaden." And with that Vera slipped back into the shadows without a sound. Not even the click of her heels could be heard against the bricks.

Kaden took a step in the same direction, but the woman was gone. There was something intriguing about her, and yet he knew her to be lethal. He hoped he hadn't said something she would use against him later on.

"Great," he muttered as he headed in for the night. "As if being under my father's thumb wasn't enough, now a mobster's daughter could come calling someday."

The following day, Frankie found herself lost again. Towering above her were thick hedges that entwined into a labyrinth of pathways that seemingly led nowhere. She'd already been up and down the rows and backtracked countless times but found herself at the same dead ends. Or at least they appeared identical. Giving up was impossible unless she planned to die out there. She wondered if someone would come looking for her if she missed another meal. She'd already skipped breakfast, but after dinner the night before, she doubted Mr. Phillips would allow Kaden to search for her. The man was probably already planning another wedding for Kaden and Julia.

So what?

Frankie knew Kaden didn't belong to her. If he wanted to marry Julia, who was she to stop him? After dinner the previous evening, she'd retreated to her room to sulk, but by morning she felt better and more embarrassed by her tantrum at the table. She skipped breakfast because she wasn't up to apologizing just yet.

Wouldn't Malcolm love that? He didn't strike her as the type to forgive and forget.

Poor Kaden. He had been so close to living his dream in Alaska. If only Vera had let him go.

More and more, Frankie disliked her mother, and after her behavior at dinner, her scorn for Vera had tripled. What had Papa seen in her? She was snobby and controlling and fake.

Why did Vera Cordero have to be her mother?

Why did she have to show up and ruin the motherly image Frankie had conjured up throughout her childhood? Vera was the farthest thing possible from that woman. As outraged as she'd been when she found out about it, Papa had been right to take her from Vera. Frankie couldn't imagine who she would have become if Vera had raised her.

Frankie came to another dead end in the twisted maze. She thought about calling out for help. At some point, she would have to.

Around the next corner, Frankie found a white bench and sat, shivering. The whole place creeped her out. She longed for rows of apple trees instead of gothic hedges. She closed her eyes and imagined her farm. She envisioned her mountains and even the lake that had always scared her. She had never had any reason to fear it. As far as Frankie knew, her mother had never even set foot on that land.

Frankie didn't know what was worse—believing her mother died at the lake or wishing she would simply disappear, never to show up in her daughter's life again.

She dropped her face into her hands and rested her elbows on her knees. She hated thinking such thoughts, but if Vera meant to kill her, Frankie couldn't feel bad about wishing the old story had remained in place.

A rustling sound dragged Frankie's attention to the right. "Hello?" she called out.

No answer.

Maybe she had imagined it. Wishful thinking that Kaden had come to find her. Not that he would.

But then she heard it again and jumped to her feet. Someone was definitely getting closer. "Is someone there? Kaden? I can't find my way out of this maze. I could use some help."

"Would you take mine?" Vera came into view.

Frankie took a step back, and her calves hit the bench. She glanced in the opposite direction, trying to gauge whether she could run.

"I don't mean you any harm." Vera's words stopped her. They went against everything Frankie had witnessed thus far.

"How do I know you're telling the truth?"

"I suppose you don't. It will be a risk. But I think you're up for taking it. From what I've seen, my daughter is braver than I first believed.

I misjudged you, and I'm sorry. Can we sit and talk for a bit?" Vera gestured to the bench with a wave of her hand.

Frankie took a deep breath and dropped down on the edge of the stone, her hands curled around the seat, ready to spring into action if she had to.

"This is the first time we've been alone together since you were an infant. You were a doll. My sweet Francesca." Vera smiled down at her hands, folded on her lap. She lifted her face and said, "And now you are my brave Frankie."

Frankie shifted uncomfortably on the bench, trying not to let Vera's words suck her in. She imagined a tangled web as deceiving as the maze. But Vera's web included men with guns. The only way to combat the situation was by arming herself with the truth.

"Why didn't you come with Papa and me when we went into the Witness Security Program?" The question spilled from her lips with ease. It was what she wanted to know most of all. There could be nothing between her and her mother until that question was answered.

Vera sat with her back straight as an arrow, her poise and elegance surpassing anything Frankie had ever seen. Without checking her bank account records, Frankie knew Vera was the real deal. She didn't need the cherubs on the front gate or the hall of past aristocrats to display her wealth. And no matter how hard Frankie tried, she couldn't imagine her mother sitting on top of a tractor. She was so feminine with her perfectly coiffed hair in its artful twist. Her pristine manner with her manicured nails made Frankie ashamed of her own calloused and tan hands. Her nails were blunt, and she found a speck of dirt still under them. She picked at it as she waited for a response.

As Frankie's question hung in the air for minutes with no answer, she began to suspect that she wouldn't get one. Which meant there was nothing else to say.

Frankie stood to leave, but before she could take one step, her mother caught her hand.

Vera lifted her face and with watering eyes, said, "I love your father more than life itself."

Love? As in present tense?

Vera's statement stunned Frankie, and she froze in her spot. She wondered if her father knew, and if he felt the same way. He hadn't answered her question the night before.

"Then why didn't you go with him? With me?"

A slow smile spread across Vera's face. She searched Frankie's eyes and took both her hands into her own. "He has done an amazing job raising you. I know now that I made the right choice."

"Abandoning me was the right choice?"

Even Vera's frown was beautiful. Papa always told Frankie that she resembled her mother, but Frankie couldn't see it. She doubted that would change even if she donned Vera's classy dress and heels.

"I could give you excuse after excuse," Vera said. "My own mother had just passed away. My father's heavy hand kept me working for the family business. My family would not have let me go willingly, and most likely would have killed me, or all three of us. I let obligations come before love. They would all be valid reasons, but the truth is, they would be excuses. The real reason is that I feared I would raise you to be another me. I knew even if Daniel took me away from a life of organized crime, he would never be able to get the stain of it off me."

"And you weren't willing to try."

"I was sure you would be better off without me, and I was afraid. When I realized you both were gone, I wept for weeks, but not only from losing you. I cried over the guilt of my relief. My father wanted to go after you, but I stopped him. Deep down, I knew Daniel had made the choice I should have, but couldn't. He gave you a life of freedom I could never have. My father would have never stopped hunting us."

Her use of the word hunt darkened the conversation. After seeing Greg's body and Winnie's betrayal, Frankie felt the heaviness of such a word. She realized her mother had grown up in that dark world without any hope of escape.

"What did you do in your family business?" It was a loaded question, and Frankie probably would not like the answer. She braced herself.

"Nothing as sinister as you're thinking." Vera smiled up at her. But her smile quickly vanished. "I mostly ran the books for our construction business."

"Bookkeeping?" Had Frankie found something in common with her mother? Her father had said the same thing, but she'd been afraid to believe it. "I went to school for accounting."

Vera's smile returned, more brightly than before. "You did? How lovely. I don't know about you, but my mind thinks in patterns and numbers."

"I'm not sure about patterns," Frankie said, moving to reclaim her seat. "But when something involves numbers and organization, it comes naturally to me. I keep the books for the farm and have our whole inventory of supplies cataloged. I brought my ledger if you want to see it."

"I would like that. Perhaps someday."

"Someday?"

Vera tightened her grasp on Frankie's hand. "I'm going to get you out of this. But that means I have to leave again. I'm going to attempt to lead my brother away from you."

Less than an hour before, Frankie would not have minded the abrupt, jarring announcement. "But we found something we have in common," she said, knowing it sounded pathetic and not caring. "I want to know what else there is."

"And I love that. I love you, and I always have." Vera pressed her lips together and took a deep breath. "When I was pregnant with you, I knew you deserved a better life than I could give you. I was keeping the books for my father's construction and real estate business. But I became ill and Daniel had to take over the books. He was my dad's foreman on the construction sites, but he also had a keen mind for numbers. When he took over the bookkeeping, everything unraveled. My father was a ruthless businessman, but Cameron, my brother, was a killer. As Daniel was keeping the books, he brought an irregularity to my attention."

Her eyes closed. "I knew my brother had done something horrible. Out of fear, I asked Daniel to forget what he saw. I wish I had been braver, like you were last night at dinner. But I wasn't, and soon the feds came knocking and threatened to put me away as an accomplice. Thanks to your father's sacrifice, I didn't go to jail, but Cameron did. When word came that he was being released, I knew he would hunt down you and Daniel. I did some digging and found that he had already hired people and was two steps ahead of me. I hacked into Cameron's personal bank account and found the mole that he had placed in the U.S. Marshals' Seattle office. Then I had to wait and pray that Daniel would get you there."

"Papa told me about all that. But it wasn't him who got me to the office. It was Kaden."

Vera's eyes lit up. "Kaden is a good man. I actually recognize myself in him quite a bit. I know his turmoil." She stood and scanned the hedges around them. "It's a pattern. Two lefts and a right."

Frankie realized her mother was giving her directions out of the maze. "Of course. Why didn't I see it?"

Vera took Frankie's hand and pulled her up gently from the seat. "Sometimes we're too close to see the bigger picture. And when we're in the thick of it, all we see is the obstacles before us. I'm going to get you out of this, Frankie. I promise."

Hand in hand, Frankie and her mother walked through the maze until they stepped out of the labyrinth, free from its clutches.

"Will I see you again?" Frankie asked.

"Perhaps someday." Vera leaned in and kissed Frankie on the cheek. "Do whatever you have to in order to stay alive."

"It's not fair. I just met you. We haven't had a chance to get to know each other at all."

"I learned a long time ago that life isn't fair. It's about surviving. Survive, Francesca. Then all of this will have been worth it."

Hearing her name on her mother's lips made her feel comforted, despite everything. She did her best to memorize the sound, imprinting it on her brain in case their paths never crossed again. She could tell her mother wanted to give her a hug, but she squeezed Frankie's hand instead, clearly unsure of herself.

Frankie stepped in and wrapped her arms around her mother to give her the hug they both longed for.

"You are more than I ever imagined," Vera murmured to her. "More than I ever could be."

Frankie focused on memorizing her mother's fragrance, which spoke of wealth, whereas Frankie wore the smell of a simple farm girl.

"Don't ever change," Vera added in little more than a whisper.

Frankie let her mother slip from her grasp as she closed her eyes, carving into her mind the feel and aroma of Vera Cordero.

Her mother, whom she'd barely found before losing her again.

16

*K*aden prepped for Saturday evening's dinner, selecting clothes from a closet filled with suits and formal wear. As he removed a navy-blue suit he hadn't worn in months and laid it on his bed, he realized his father had chosen his whole wardrobe. He also knew Frankie would once again have nothing that met his parents' approval at the dining room table.

He smiled, thinking about their response to her overalls the previous evening. She was putting them in their place, and she didn't even realize it. He envied that self-assuredness in her. Her bravery came out effortlessly and unapologetically.

He could learn a lot from her if he had the guts. Learning was one thing, carrying it out was where he faltered. As he stared at his suit coat, Kaden had a sudden vision of what the rest of his life would be like if he didn't make significant changes.

A life under his father's endless oppression.

He didn't know what, if anything, would come of his relationship with Frankie. What he did know was that being around her intrigued him enough to find out. What he did know was that a world without her would be devastating. She was a breath of fresh air, unblemished by the bitterness so many people seemed to carry. He knew she would walk into the formal dining room later that night in a pair of jeans, a T-shirt, and her cowgirl boots, and he would fall for her all over again, even harder than if she appeared in a fine ball gown.

Kaden felt like a piece of rope with his father on one end and Frankie on the other, playing a game of tug-of-war. But with each pull, Kaden prayed Frankie would win.

Except he hadn't given her any reason to try. At what point would she drop the rope and walk away?

Kaden had to prove to her that he was worth her trouble. And he realized he could do that with a simple pair of jeans.

He dug through his closet for a clean pair of jeans, a white T-shirt, and a red flannel shirt. He didn't own a pair of cowboy boots—something he planned to rectify—but he had a pair of hiking boots from a trip he'd taken to Lake Tahoe. He readied for dinner with a smile, building his strength with each article of clothing he donned. A glance in the mirror on his way out the door showed a man worthy of Frankie's attention. A man who wasn't afraid of the hard work it would take to be worthy of her.

Kaden made his way through the house until he entered the dining room, seeking the only approval he needed.

His feet stopped along with his heart when he saw her.

"Frankie?" The sight before him made no sense.

She stood by the fire, dressed in a long green cocktail dress that draped off her shoulders in sheer elegance. The waistline cinched in a ruffle at her left hip, and the fabric cascaded down to the floor. One foot protruded out, showing a pair of black heels.

What happened to her boots? Kaden thought. Not that he was complaining at all. She was stunning, no matter what she wore.

"Good evening, Kaden. Nice of you to join us for dinner. You're late." She grinned and recaptured his heart.

So much for thinking I wouldn't like her in a gown.

"You look amazing. But where did you get the dress?"

"My mother left it for me."

He scanned the room. "Where is she? I must thank her."

Before Frankie answered his question, Chris stepped into the dining room, clearly frazzled and not ready for dinner. "I seem to have misplaced my wife. Has anyone seen her lately?"

"Oh, Papa." Frankie crossed the room toward her father.

Kaden remained with his mother, but by the devastation on Chris's face, he knew Frankie had told him Vera was gone.

Unable to gather the particulars with his parents so close by, he guessed that Vera was acting as a decoy to steer the Cordero family and their hired help away from them. Distraught, Chris left the room, leaving Frankie to stand alone, hiding her own pain.

"I don't know what is going on around here," his mother said beside him. "What happened to Vera? She's the one member of that family with any couth." She gave Kaden a once-over. "And why are you dressed like that? Go change right this minute."

"No." The word slipped from his lips before he could catch them. As his mother's face reddened, Kaden felt a bubble of joy roll up within him and spill from his lips in a laugh.

His mother's mouth dropped in disgust. She huffed and called to her husband, "Your son needs a reminder of the way we do things here."

Malcolm stepped forward from where he had been talking to the butler. "I heard from Julia's parents today that you have not called her. Explain yourself."

"There's nothing to explain. I wasn't ready, and frankly, I'm never going to be ready. Julia and I will never be married. You need to understand that."

"So we're back to this again. I'll have you know that her parents are drawing up the agreement as we speak."

Kaden saw his life play out before his eyes. From suits to marriage contracts, his father's plans felt inevitable and inexorable. Kaden's refusal stuck on his tongue.

Frankie watched him, waiting for him to make his decision. When he gave no response, she spun away from him and headed toward the door.

"Wait." He rushed forward to catch her at the door, but even in heels, she stayed ahead of him.

"Kaden Gerard Phillips, you will return to this dining room immediately," Malcolm ordered.

"Never!" he shouted as he ran to the hallway, watching Frankie burst through the glass doors to the patio and disappear into the hedges. "Frankie, wait!"

The setting sun cast shadows through the garden, and in her green dress, he almost missed her and ran right past. Stopping abruptly, he returned with his arms out.

"I'm so sorry," he said sincerely. "I need you to know you mean the world to me. I want to be worthy of your love."

"What do you mean?"

"You already know. I have fallen in love with you. You are like no one I have ever met, and I can't imagine ever being away from you. But I haven't been worthy of you. I've been afraid."

She took a step forward with her hand out. "Don't be."

It was all the encouragement Kaden needed to bridge the gap between them and take her in his arms. He kissed her gently.

"Kaden, what are we going to do? We can't stay here."

All he could do was shake his head, knowing it could be the last moment they saw each other. Beyond the gates, killers hunted her, and Kaden had unleashed the wrath of his father inside the house. She was right. Their time there was over.

"We'll leave in the morning," he whispered. "Tell your father—"

"He's gone."

"What? Where? We just saw him."

"He went after Vera. As soon as I told him what she planned, he became more determined than I've ever seen him. He loves her. He really does. And she loves him."

"But he left you here alone."

"No. He left me with you. He trusts you to protect me."

The weight of expectation nearly crippled him. "What if I fail?"

She beamed at him. "Both my parents have faith in you. And so do I. We'll leave in the morning like you said."

"You humble me," he said. "I don't deserve—"

"Stop. Yes, you do. You've proven time and time again that you will stand by my side, that together we will get through this."

Kaden dropped his forehead to hers and nodded. "Together. I like that. Wherever that may be, we'll go together."

Her eyes filled. "Alaska? Can we still do that?"

"I don't know. Without my plane, I'm grounded. My father even owns my car. We'll take it in the morning until we can get another one. I think we need to go to the police, though."

"Papa never trusted them, but I suppose he had his reasons." She slid a small green purse from her shoulder and pulled a tissue from it to blot her teary eyes. "Okay, I'll follow your lead. Tomorrow morning, we'll leave and go to the police." She started to close the purse—then stopped and opened it wider. "There's another compartment in this."

"Is this your mother's as well?"

"Yes. She left the dress, the shoes, and the purse on my bed." Frankie unzipped the compartment and gasped. "There's cash in here." Her eyes grew wide as she reached in to remove the bills. "Kaden, I've never seen so much money in my life."

A quick count of the cash came out to five thousand dollars. He smiled at her innocence and loved how even money had no hold on her. The money wouldn't get them far, but it would be a start.

"Thank you, Vera," he said.

"Yeah, thank you, Mama." Frankie stashed the money back in the hidden compartment. "When do we leave?"

"Be ready before dawn. I'll tap on your door. I would leave now, but we would be stopped before we reached the gate. And if we happened to make it beyond that, Cordero's men would see us."

"I hope my mother's plan worked and they are long gone."

"Me too. But we're going to get out of here either way." Hope filled him, and he felt braver than he ever had in his life. In Frankie's arms, he felt strong and ready to take on anyone and anything that came their way.

Belief was half the battle, but would it be enough?

17

Shortly before sunrise Sunday morning, Frankie and Kaden sneaked down the back stairway and into the garage. Once again, she carried her backpack with her few belongings and her mother's picture. Brokenhearted about not taking another one with her when they spoke in the garden, Frankie vowed to hold onto that one for dear life.

"We'll take the most inconspicuous car here," Kaden said, opening a safe to remove a set of keys.

"How many cars does Malcolm have?"

"Ten." He led her through a heavy metal door, flipping on the lights to reveal the ten vehicles.

"Wow. These are beautiful. I don't know what they all are, but they look fast."

"We need fast. But I also don't want anything bright." Kaden approached a large gray car. "We'll take this one. It's what I typically drive around town, so I'm familiar with it. My father won't miss it right away either. It's not pretentious enough for him."

"Well, I like it." She opened the passenger door and climbed into leather seats that felt like a buttery cocoon. "This beats Papa's old truck any day."

Kaden chuckled as he started the engine. "Seeing you drive that old truck was quite attractive, I must admit."

"Can't be as attractive as seeing you behind this wheel."

He leaned over and kissed her quickly. Time was short, but she would take his kisses as often as she could get them.

"Buckle up," he whispered, and smiled close to her lips.

She kissed him one more time and reached for the seat belt.

"We'll head into town and go straight to the police station." Kaden opened the garage door and pulled the vehicle out of the bay. Frankie was grateful the engine was quieter than she had expected. "I'll keep an eye on my rearview mirror for anyone following us from the side. You do the same on yours."

Frankie nodded, unable to speak as the weight of the endeavor sank in. They were on their own, and no backup would be coming for them.

Do whatever you have to in order to stay alive.

Frankie had to hope her mother's attempt to lure the criminals away had worked.

Kaden hit the button to open the gates, which didn't require a code to leave, then slid the car out onto the street.

Frankie craned her neck to peer behind them, but there was no sign of a tail. "Nothing yet," she said. "Do you see anyone?"

"Not at all. Keep watching though."

"The Corderos won't know what car we have. Plus, Vera led them away yesterday." Nausea rolled through her at the thought of what the Cordero thugs might do to her mother when they found out she had tricked them.

Kaden followed the river and drove through some older suburbs with prominent houses. When he finally came to a downtown area, he pulled the car into an angled parking space on the side of the road.

Storefronts and boutiques lined both sides of the street, and on any other day, Frankie would have loved to window-shop. "What a cute town."

"We probably should get some clothes and necessities for the trip after we stop at the police station. I'm hoping they can look into the U.S. Marshals' whereabouts." He gestured to a brick building on the next block. "That's the station there."

"Sounds like a plan," Frankie said, opening her door carefully. She scanned the area before stepping out, then made her way to the sidewalk.

"Kaden?" a feminine voice called from behind them as Kaden stepped onto the sidewalk beside Frankie.

Spinning around, Frankie found a woman with long, straight blonde hair jogging across the street and straight for them. She was tall, slender, and dressed in running clothes that fit her like a glove. If she was out exercising, she didn't break a sweat.

"Do you know her?" Frankie asked warily.

"It's Julia," Kaden said. "She and I need to talk."

"Okay," Frankie agreed, unease twisting inside her.

Julia launched herself into Kaden's arms, squealing in delight. "I heard you were back. Why haven't you called me?"

"There wasn't much time. I'm not staying."

Julia pouted. "You're still flying to Alaska?"

"We're not sure yet."

"We?" Julia glanced in Frankie's direction for the first time, then back at Kaden as she processed the new information.

"Julia, this is Frankie. Frankie, this is Julia, my ex-fiancée."

Frankie wasn't sure how to approach the new territory. Was it always so awkward when the new girlfriend met the old one?

And am I even Kaden's girlfriend?

She extended her hand. "It's nice to meet you, Julia."

Julia appeared stunned but took Frankie's hand and shook it slowly. She gaped at Kaden. "I don't believe it. You leave town for less than two weeks and fall in love? Wait until my parents hear this."

Frankie had to say something. She couldn't bear the idea of causing Kaden more trouble than she already had. "It's not what you think."

Kaden interrupted. "Yes it is. I do love her."

Julia squealed and hugged Kaden again, then did the same with Frankie. "I am so happy for you both. She's beautiful."

When she pulled back, Frankie could see Julia held no animosity toward her at all. In fact, it was the opposite. She was obviously as happy for Kaden as she claimed. Genuinely thrilled that he found someone to bring him joy.

Julia reached for his arm. "But we need to talk about my parents and yours. They are on a crusade. They're so obsessed with getting us married."

"I know. I'm trying to get out of town right now," Kaden explained. "We're kind of on the run."

"On the run? Did you break the law?" Julia asked, eyes wide.

"Nothing like that. Don't worry." Kaden scanned the street, and Frankie followed suit.

So far, there was no sign of anyone following them.

Kaden took her hand. "Frankie, would you mind hanging out in the bookstore while I talk to Julia for a few minutes? Then we can go."

"Sure."

He placed a kiss on her lips and murmured, "Don't go anywhere else. I'll come back for you. We're going to go for a walk to sort things out. Give me ten minutes."

Frankie nodded, unable to speak after such a public display of affection. She stepped inside the bookstore and watched the two of them cross the street to a little café with black garden tables outside. She knew she didn't have anything to worry about—after all, Kaden had already established with Julia that he loved Frankie, and Julia had been excited for them.

"Can I help you?" an employee asked her.

Frankie touched her lips where Kaden had kissed her. She wanted to tell the employee that Kaden loved her, but why would the young woman care? Still, Frankie wanted to shout it from the rooftops.

Instead, she took a deep breath and said, "I'm browsing."

"Sure thing. Let me know if you need any help." The woman climbed a ladder to return a book to a top shelf.

The bookstore was warm and welcoming, permeated by a relaxing aroma of mahogany and paper. Built-in shelves lined the walls, and stand-alone bookshelves formed a maze on the floor.

Frankie meandered her way through each row, not really paying attention to what the bookstore had to offer. Every so often, the bell over the door rang, and the employee offered each customer the same help she'd offered Frankie. At the back of the store, Frankie ran her fingertips over various titles, coming to a stop on a book about organized crime.

Her stomach clenched at the words, and she pulled the volume from the shelf and leafed through it.

The book was about a particular family, and photographs filled the pages as words described their criminal exploits. She came to a chapter about the wives and children of the mobsters, and she peeked into what her life would have been like if Papa hadn't taken her out of that world.

Beneath the gaudy jewelry and glamorous dresses, Frankie gazed into their eyes and found nothing. Not even a semblance of life, of humanity left. How had her mother lived in that world and retained her dignity?

Frankie snapped the book shut, not wanting to have anything to do with the mob. More than ever, she was grateful that her father had saved her from it. Who would she have been if she had remained? Would she be one of the alluring women in fur coats and fashionable dresses? Frankie was more in awe of her mother than ever. Her mother hadn't been able to break free, but neither had her family succeeded in breaking her spirit.

Frankie returned the book to the shelf and found the employee she'd spoken to earlier. "Can you help me find a book?"

"It would be my pleasure. Which book are you looking for?"

"Something on Alaska. I might be moving there."

"All our travel books are on this side of the store." The woman gestured. "You'll find Alaska under the A's."

Frankie easily located a row of books about the northernmost state. She selected one and opened it in the middle. The rugged terrain and mountain peaks captured her fascination in an instant. The expansive openness of the land returned a peace to her that the mob book had stolen.

Could Alaska be her future?

She knew it would make Kaden happy, and if he was happy, she would be too. As much as she longed for Nighthawk Farm, she had to let that go. Her farm had been a hiding place, and it was time to stop hiding.

Frankie took the book to the checkout counter and paid for it with some of the money her mother had left her. It felt right, even though she knew they would need money to survive. She planned to devour the book and fall in love with the place because Kaden loved it.

The bell above the door rang, and a man in a black suit stepped inside and took an immediate right to a bookshelf.

"Enjoy your time in Alaska," the employee said as she dropped the book into a bag.

Aware that people in the store could be listening, Frankie simply smiled.

"You'll love it," the woman gushed. "I spent some time near Anchorage for the summer. I had an aunt who lived there, and she invited me to stay and help out at her farm."

"Farm?" Frankie suddenly felt that everything was going to be okay. The bell rang again. "That sounds lovely."

"It was. Enjoy your time there, and enjoy your book." The woman greeted the next customer in line.

As Frankie stepped outside onto the sidewalk, she glanced across the street to where she'd last seen Kaden and Julia.

But the seats were empty.

Kaden had told her to stay where she was, that he would come and get her. His car was still where he'd parked it. Perhaps they were sitting inside it for privacy.

She walked to the edge of the storefront, trying to see through the sun's glare on the windshield.

A hand snaked into her vision and clamped over her mouth. The barrel of a gun dug into her ribs.

She tried to struggle, but a bristly cheek scraped against hers. "Don't move," growled the person holding her. "We're going to do this nice and easy."

He yanked her into the alley.

She screamed into the rough hand over her mouth, dropping her bag to pry at his grip. His fingers moved up to pinch her nostrils without releasing her mouth, cutting off her air and making her dizzy. He dragged her through the alley as she kicked and fought for air. At the other end of the alley, a car screeched to a halt and the rear door opened. Frankie's captor hurled her inside, and she landed on the floor in a heap, gasping for breath.

She caught her first glimpse of the man as he took the seat beside her and shut the door. He had the same eyes as the criminals in the book—blank, with nothing in them.

She tried to scream for help, but the car took off before she could make so much as a squeak.

All Frankie knew was that Kaden would never find her, and if the man who'd kidnapped her was anything like the others, she prayed for his sake that Kaden wouldn't try.

18

$\mathcal{K}$aden and Julia sat in the police station after spending the previous hour scouring the area for Frankie. Trying to get the police to take her disappearance seriously was proving to be fruitless. They gave him a whole spiel about a person having to be missing for twenty-four hours before they could start a search. Even after Kaden explained the circumstances, most of the officers rolled their eyes at the idea of the mob having kidnapped Frankie.

Thankfully, he convinced a couple of them to at least help him search. She couldn't have gone far on her own two feet.

But after going through every store, he slumped back into a chair at the police station and attempted to stop his mind from going to worst-case scenarios.

"We'll find her," Julia said reassuringly. But she didn't understand who they were up against.

"I've seen what they do to people. I saw it with my own eyes. All I can hope is that Frankie's still alive." His voice cracked and he dropped his face into his hands.

"Maybe she's shopping," Julia offered hopefully.

"We checked in all the stores."

Julia's typical bright smile dimmed. Even she knew she was grasping at straws.

An officer stepped into the waiting room. "Mr. Phillips? I have a few questions I'd like to go over with you."

"Did you find her?"

"Not yet, but some of my best men are out there, so rest assured we'll get to the bottom of this. But I'm a little concerned about who this woman is. None of the names you've given me register. It's as if she doesn't exist."

"I told you," he said, trying not to groan with frustration. "She was in witness protection. Her original name was Francesca Paparella. It was changed to Francesca Stiles."

The officer shook his head. "Neither of those names give me anything. Are you sure she hasn't been taking you for a ride?"

"I don't know what you mean."

Something too close to pity ranged over the officer's features. "Is it possible she was conning you?"

"No. Not a chance. Frankie is as genuine as they come. Her name must've been erased when we were at the U.S. Marshals' office in Seattle. You can call and ask them."

"That's not information they give out on the phone, for obvious reasons, but I'll put in a call. Are you absolutely certain she didn't leave you on purpose?"

"Do you think it's possible that she left under the impression I wanted to be with you instead?" Kaden asked Julia.

"No way," she replied. "I didn't let her believe that was an option."

"I agree. No, she wouldn't have left on purpose," he told the officer. "She knew the danger out there. We have to find her before it's too late."

The officer returned to his desk and picked up the phone.

The double doors at the entrance opened, and two officers stepped inside. One carried a white plastic bag. "We found this book in the alley and spoke to the bookstore owner. The woman at the checkout desk said a woman fitting Frankie's description bought this book a little over an hour ago."

Kaden jumped to his feet. "Let me see." The officer handed him the bag, and he pulled out a small coffee-table volume. "She bought a book on Alaska?" He was touched that she would do such a thing. Even under the circumstances, his Frankie was hopeful. "Which alley was it? We'll head down there and see if we can retrace her steps."

"Her steps ceased at the end of the alley. There's evidence of foul play, and we can tell she was dragged. Tire marks show that a car came to a sharp stop at the other end of the alley from the bookstore, so she was probably loaded into it. I want to get our forensics team out there and process the street where the car was and the alleyway for any evidence of who might have taken her."

As the officers went to work on the crime scene, Kaden spiraled with worry. With each passing moment, the chances of Frankie remaining alive diminished. There was no time to pull prints or search for hairs or DNA on the off chance that something might produce a lead.

He dropped back into the seat, clutching the book to his chest. It was the last thing Frankie had held. If only she had stayed inside the store. He loved her innocence, but in the end, it was her innocence and trust in people that had gotten her abducted.

It was her trust in him.

"I tried to tell her not to trust me," he muttered. "That I wasn't up for this. She believed in me, and now she's gone."

Julia nudged him. "She was right to believe in you. You can't blame yourself. Neither of you were prepared for such awful people. Do you know who they are? Like do you have names and faces and locations?"

"Boston. It's the Cordero family that has been after her. Well, after her father." A spark of hope jolted Kaden, and he faced Julia. "Maybe they'll keep her alive. They want her father. Do you think they'll keep her alive to get to him?"

"You're asking the wrong person," Julia admitted. "I don't know how mob families work."

"Neither do I, but I can't give up on her. I have to hang on to whatever hope I can come up with."

"You really love her, don't you?" Julia's eyes filled with tears. He didn't think he'd ever seen her cry.

His conscience struck him. "Does that upset you?"

"Two weeks ago, I might have been a little jealous. But seeing how different you are with her . . . All I've ever wanted was for you to be happy and to chase your dreams. It never dawned on me that your dreams would be Frankie."

Julia's words stunned Kaden into silence. All that time, he'd thought he was chasing his dreams of Alaska and freedom, but what if Julia was right?

"It's as if my plane knew where my dream was when it forced me to land at Nighthawk Farm," he said.

"And where is your dream heading now? Boston?"

"Most likely."

Julia pulled out her cell phone and made a call. "Daddy? I need your plane."

Kaden had flown with Julia numerous times in her father's private jet. They'd taken it back and forth to California during college, and they'd even planned to borrow it on their honeymoon. But it would be the first time Kaden piloted the plane himself.

"Are you sure?" he asked.

She put her finger to her lips to quiet him. "It's a matter of life and death, Daddy. We have a pilot. A very good one." She winked at Kaden.

He held his breath as he waited for Mr. Woodworth's decision. When Julia gave him a thumbs-up, the knot in his chest lessened slightly.

"Thank you, Daddy." She hung up. "I hope you can fly a jet."

He shrugged. "How hard could it be?"

"Somehow that doesn't make me feel better." She stood and gave him a little shove toward the door. "The plane is waiting on the tarmac. Go and chase your dream."

Kaden hugged her. "Thank you, my friend. I hope I find her in time."

"Me too."

Frankie stirred awake, but everything around her remained blurry. The last thing she remembered was being stuffed into a car.

No, the last thing she remembered was a drink of water from her kidnapper. *They drugged me.*

She tried to swallow, but her mouth was so dry that it hurt her throat. If she asked for more water, would they drug her again? The pain in her head, the blurry vision, and the longing to sleep kept her from figuring out her location.

She felt like her body was moving, but not in a car.

She tried to call out, but her dry throat produced no sound.

Frankie realized that she couldn't even roll over. It took her another few seconds to realize her hands were bound behind her back. She forced her eyes open and saw she was in a small room, leaning against the wall with her feet straight out in front of her. A small door, not much wider than a couple of feet, stood before her. If she managed to stand, would she want to go out through it?

Did she have a choice?

With all her might, Frankie leaned forward to try to get to her knees. Just when she thought she might do it, she fell flat on her face, bumping her head on the door. She cried out in pain.

The door opened, and two beefy hands scooped her up under her arms and dragged her out. "Welcome back, sleepyhead. Perfect timing. We've landed, and your chariot awaits."

Frankie found herself being strapped to some sort of gurney. An oxygen mask was put over her mouth, and even as she struggled, she welcomed the air into her lungs. She drifted back into a slumber but jolted awake when her gurney was pushed into an ambulance.

The images around her were distorted, and the people's faces made no sense.

"Hospital?" she croaked through the mask.

"You're going home where you've always belonged." It was a woman, dressed in scrubs and wearing a surgical mask over her mouth and nose.

Frankie zeroed in on her face, trying to identify her with her eyes. Eyes so blank and filled with nothing.

"No! Please, let me go." Her words fell on deaf ears as the ambulance sped off with its sirens blaring, appearing to all to be headed to the hospital. The driver could take her anywhere, and no one would think twice. In fact, other vehicles would get out of the way to let the ambulance pass freely.

Whoever had concocted the method of getting her out of the airport must have connections who wouldn't talk to law enforcement.

The woman in scrubs picked up a syringe and filled it with something from a vial. "You're becoming agitated. This will help you relax." She sounded so sweet and helpful, but Frankie knew she was anything but. She prayed the liquid in the vial was not deadly as the woman jabbed the syringe into her arm.

Frankie shrieked at the pain of the needle, then felt all her extremities go limp as sleep beckoned but never came. Instead, she remained awake for the ride.

When the ambulance finally stopped, the rear doors opened to reveal a well-lit garage.

"Bring her upstairs to her room. It's been waiting for her for twenty-five years."

Frankie had no idea who had spoken, but the idea of her room waiting for her made her feel warm and welcomed. She tried to reject the feeling. She had been kidnapped. She should be angry. She wanted to be livid, but whatever they'd given her made her compliant, sapped her will to resist. She was sure she would go along with anything they did to her and never put up a fight.

Somewhere in the deep recesses of her mind, she recalled a lecture in college about girls receiving drugs to make them obedient. Was that what the woman had given her?

Frankie didn't care, and tears trickled down the sides of her face and into her hair, her only way of expressing her objection to her situation.

The gurney carried her through a huge house, larger and more intricate than even Kaden's family home.

Old money.

She finally understood what Papa had meant when he described the difference between Malcolm and Denise's home and the place she found herself in. She had no doubt it was the Cordero estate in Boston.

Frankie took a deep breath and wondered if Vera was there. "Mama?" she called out.

"Soon enough, my dear," a man said from somewhere above.

Frankie tried to crane her neck to find the source of the voice, but the restraints wouldn't let her. "Who is that?"

The man pushing the gurney reminded her of a robot. He paid her no mind and moved as if he were in a trance. He wore scrubs and a mask over his face.

"Please help me," Frankie begged. "What are you going to do to me?"

If he heard her, he didn't show it. Everyone was bought and paid for and didn't dare act of their own volition. Frankie couldn't believe she had ever thought her home on the farm was a prison. She finally knew what prison really was. Her father may have kept her from the world, but he never took away her free will.

She was jostled as her carriers lifted her up a massive staircase carpeted in red. The ceiling above her was painted gold, with various images from the Renaissance period. She tried to imagine how someone had gotten up there to paint them but forced her mind back to where the men were taking her.

To the room that was waiting for her.

The men took Frankie down a long hallway, heavy wooden doors passing on both sides. She could tell the carpet was thick and plush by the way the gurney had to be pushed through.

The men came to a stop and maneuvered her into a room. She was lifted from the gurney and placed gently on a bed, a canopy draped with pale-yellow sheer fabric around her.

She found that her bindings had been removed when she lifted her hand to touch the fabric. "Soft," she murmured.

"Get some sleep, dear niece." The man's voice spoke from somewhere in the room again. "Tomorrow, you will be reinstated in your place in the family."

"Okay," she said, closing her eyes in complete, involuntary acquiescence.

19

From the time Kaden had reached the Woodworth jet to when he touched down at Logan Airport in Boston, crucial hours had passed. He almost didn't get off the ground when the FAA threatened to shut down the flight because he'd recently had an accident that was still being investigated. Kaden learned the government had his plane in their possession and had deemed the emergency landing at Nighthawk Farm not his fault. With that outcome, he finally got approval to take off.

He'd spent every second since making plans to rescue Frankie, and as he taxied to his designated spot on the Logan tarmac, he went over his next steps—namely, getting to the Boston Police Department.

If the Cordero family had placed a mole with the U.S. Marshals in Seattle, Kaden figured there had to be several with the local PD. But he also couldn't count out the department as a whole. He simply had to approach them carefully without raising red flags and bringing attention to himself.

By the time Kaden got a cab to the police station, the sun was long gone. When he entered the building, he kept his head low to remain as inconspicuous as possible. His precautions were unnecessary, given the hustle and bustle in the station. After he checked in and was instructed to take a seat, forty minutes passed before anyone noticed he was there.

"Busy night," a man observed as he sat down next to Kaden. He wore a black leather coat and had his hair pulled back in a short ponytail. "Are you waiting to be processed too?"

"Actually, I'm waiting to talk to someone about a problem," Kaden answered. "I'm a lawyer. Or I used to be. I don't practice anymore."

The man smiled. "I could use a lawyer. I was told there was a warrant out for my arrest. I came willingly, because I'm innocent."

Kaden thought back to his days in law school when he had an internship in the public defender's office. He had faced many people like the man next to him. Most insisted they were innocent, expecting Kaden to get them out of trouble scot-free so they could return to their lives of crime. But every so often, he met one who truly was innocent.

He couldn't tell which was the case with the man beside him.

"As I said, I'm not practicing anymore. But I'm sure they have good public defenders for you." Kaden gestured to the busy room. "There must be someone here who will help you."

The man leaned back, resting his head against the wall. His eyes narrowed. "You're right. I do have someone here who will help me. That guy happens to be a . . . friend of sorts." He gestured to one of the officers.

Taking in the officer's sly expression and beady eyes, Kaden knew he was not the officer to approach for help in his situation. "How about the one to his right? The plainclothes one. Would he help?" Kaden whispered out of the side of his mouth.

The man scoffed. "Not likely. He's a detective and once tried to lock me up for ten years."

"For what?"

The guy gave him a wolfish grin and refused to answer.

Kaden stood. "Listen—a word of advice from a nonpracticing attorney. Your buddy isn't doing you any favors. Eventually, you will have to face whatever problems you're having. I wish you luck. Have a good night."

Kaden walked away, knowing from his public-defender days that his little pep talk was unlikely to work, but he had to try.

Much like he couldn't wait any longer to be called back. He had to jump into the bullpen and find a trustworthy cop. He approached a man reading something on his computer screen.

"Excuse me. Detective Mehlman, is it?" Kaden tried to read the name placard beneath a stack of files.

The detective shook his hand. "Yes, I'm Detective Rick Mehlman. How can I help you?" He spoke in a thick Boston accent.

"I'd like to talk to you about a certain family in the area." Kaden picked up a pen and a yellow notepad. He wrote *Cordero* on it and slid it over to the policeman.

Mehlman immediately crumpled up the paper in his hand, scanning his surroundings. "Wow, you're either brave or stupid. Who did you say you were?"

"I didn't."

Mehlman leaned back in his chair and twisted a gold band around his finger. After a few moments, he said casually, "If you're setting me up, you've picked the wrong cop to mess with."

"Not at all. I need some help. My girlfriend's been kidnapped," Kaden said. "Going to the wrong cop could get her killed. I'm hoping you're the right one."

Mehlman's face pinched in anger. "I knew this was going to happen." The detective picked up his desk phone and punched in a set of numbers. "It's started. The guy hasn't even been out for a month. Meet me in half an hour." He hung up the phone with a clatter that made the base ding and glanced up at Kaden. "I'll meet you at the corner bar. Come to the back." He went back to his computer, typing furiously.

In half an hour, Kaden would know if he'd picked the wrong cop or not.

When Frankie fully awoke it was well after noon on Monday. She still felt a bit groggy but believed the drugs had largely worn off. She vaguely remembered being carried into the bedchamber the night she arrived and wondered if it had been her bedroom as an infant. If she had remained in the home, would she have grown up in the princess-worthy room?

She checked the door and found it locked, so she wandered around, inspecting various trinkets. Had all of them been in there when she was a baby? Where had her crib stood? She liked to think the yellow remained the same. Perhaps that was why she was drawn to the color as an adult.

Frankie approached a tall wardrobe and twisted the knob to open it. Surprised to see it full of clothing, she ran her hand across a few blouses and paused on a yellow dress.

Are these my mother's clothes?

She leaned in and brought the fabric to her face to inhale, trying to pick up her mother's signature scent.

"Good, you're awake." A voice captured her attention, and she spun around to the open door.

"Who are you?" As soon as the words left her mouth, she knew the answer.

"I'm your family," replied her uncle, Cameron Cordero. "And family means everything."

"You kidnapped me from mine," she snapped. "If you believe that, then send me back."

"You're mistaken, my dear niece. It was Paparella who kidnapped you from us first. I'm righting the wrong by bringing you home."

She gazed around the beautiful room and suddenly hated it.

"This is not my home. It will never be."

"We'll see about that. Come. I'll give you the grand tour." When she hesitated, he added sharply, "Now," and she didn't dare disobey.

If she thought her bedroom was beautiful, it was nothing compared to the rest of the place. It made Kaden's family's home look like a guesthouse. The Cordero house was decorated in rich golds and reds. Original artwork, not prints, adorned the walls. There were nooks and crannies galore, and when they reached a great room, her uncle tugged on a book, and a whole bookshelf opened to reveal an office.

"This is where we keep our secret books," he said. "You'll be spending a lot of time in here. I did some digging and found that you've been running that farm for some time, and quite successfully. I'm impressed with your abilities. But like mother like daughter, I suppose. This is where Vera worked as well. Her loss, your gain."

The idea of her mother being forced to work in a secret chamber for so many years made her ill. The realization that Cameron was expecting her to do the same made her want to run. But where?

Frankie lifted her chin with more bravado than she felt. "If you have to keep your books in a secret passage, then you must make your money by corruption. I will have no part of that."

"Not all of it, and yes, you will." He exited and waited for her to follow, swinging the bookshelf back into place behind her. He continued the tour, acting as though she had paid for admission to the place. They came to another hallway, and Cameron stopped. "You should hope you're never taken down this hallway. I call it The Last Mile."

Frankie saw a single door at the far end of the hall. She didn't have to be told what horrors it led to. She saw firsthand what the Corderos did to anyone they no longer had use for.

"Did you kill Greg or did you have someone else do it?" she asked quietly.

"We have people for that. But I am sorry about your neighbor. My men followed the tracker right to him. It was supposed to lead them to your father instead. Your neighbor was unfortunate collateral damage, but he'd seen the drone's footage."

Frankie didn't dare ask whether her father was still alive. She didn't want to know the answer.

But Cameron told her anyway. "I expect Paparella to arrive soon and become my next voyager down The Last Mile."

Frankie quietly prayed against it. She hoped her father was far away and would never return.

"What about my mother?"

Cameron shook his head in mock sadness. "She nearly ruined all my plans to find you. She'll have to pay for that. And to think I believed her crocodile tears when you were taken as a baby. My sister is such a good actress." He patted his lean stomach. "I don't know about you, but I am famished. Brunch is on the veranda. Let's dine."

Frankie reluctantly followed him through the rest of the house and out onto a large stone veranda. Numerous steps led onto a large courtyard the size of a football field. She took it all in as she approached a round table loaded with food. Cameron held her chair out for her, and she remembered her words to Kaden. Could she say them to Cameron?

Did she dare?

She squared her shoulders. "I can get my own chair. I've been doing it my whole life."

"The way you've lived your life is over. Now sit. We have business to discuss."

Frankie bit her tongue and took the seat. "What sort of business?"

"As I told you inside, you'll be taking over the books that my sister left behind. I expect to continue the business that my father left to me in the will. Did you know that you were also in his will?"

Frankie shook her head. "Why?"

Cameron began scooping food onto her plate. "Sadly, I can't have children. When you were born, it was made clear to all of us that you would be the heir of the Cordero estate. After you were kidnapped as an infant, my father kept you in the will with the hope that you would be found someday and restored to your rightful place among us. Then, on his deathbed, he took you out of the will. I was in prison at the time, thanks to your father, but when I heard you'd been removed, I knew something was up."

"It doesn't matter. I don't want any of this. You can have it all."

Cameron laughed. "That's not an option. Anyway, to continue my story before I was so rudely interrupted, I knew something was up. I had eyes out and discovered that Vera knew you were alive and where you were. She convinced our father to take you out of the will before he died, thinking that when I was released, I would be pleased and never go after you. She was wrong. Like I said, family is everything."

"And what about my family? Like my father?"

"He's not Cordero blood. You are. End of story. You should hate your father. He stole you from your inheritance. But I can fix it with a swipe of a pen."

"I don't want your blood money."

Cameron laughed again. "You are so like your mother. But if Vera could be whipped into shape, so can you." He caressed her cheek with the back of his hand.

Frankie swallowed hard as her body revolted against the gesture.

Vera had been right. Cameron Cordero was a killer. Whether he killed with his own hands or ordered someone else to do his dirty work, the man was a monster.

"I'll leave you to your meal. I'm not hungry anymore." Cameron stood and strode inside through the glass doors. That was when she noticed the guards standing on either side. Her every move would be watched from then on.

She began to understand the life her mother could never escape, the reason Vera had let Papa take their daughter into the program. But it had all been for nothing.

Frankie was officially a prisoner.

Ignoring the food Cameron had served her, she stood and picked an apple out of a bowl. To test her boundaries, she trotted down the steps and out onto the courtyard. She glanced back to see the men had moved to stand at the bottom of the stairs. She walked across the vast lawn and came to a reflective pool. Within a few minutes, their reflection wavered in the water as well, with their hands clasped before them. She wondered if they would live in her room too.

She would never be free again.

Gazing into the reflective pool, she pictured her rows of fruit trees and her horse, Shadow, who loved apples. She let her mind wander to that peaceful place and pretended she was there again.

Frankie explored toward the edge of the property. Tall hedges blocked her view, their leaves rustling in the wind. She lifted her face to feel the breeze—but there wasn't one. The air was heavy and still.

She did a double take and caught sight of a pair of eyes she would recognize anywhere.

Kaden hid in the foliage of the hedge.

Frankie's heart rate picked up, both with excitement at his presence and with terror for his life. If Kaden was caught, he would be taken to The Last Mile her uncle had warned her about. She shook her head slightly to tell Kaden to stay away. She imagined her mother had felt the same fear before Papa had disappeared into witness protection with their baby.

Save yourself, she begged him silently. *Run far away and don't ever look back. Run, Kaden. Run far away.*

As if he heard her thoughts, he vanished.

She released a deep breath and hoped he would never return, though grief wrenched her heart. He couldn't help her. She had to handle the fight herself.

She had an idea of how she could bring down Cameron. She had an inkling of where she could hit him hard and hurt him the most.

His wallet.

Her back ramrod straight, Frankie addressed the men who were her guards. "Take me to my mother's office. If this is what I'm going to do for a living, I need to learn the ropes."

Both men smiled, obviously pleased with her choice. "Right this way, Miss Cordero."

Frankie wanted to correct them about her last name, but at present, she realized that she didn't have one. Her father's original surname, Paparella, was no longer safe. Neither was the name she'd grown up with, Stiles, which wasn't even hers anyway. She wanted nothing to do with the Cordero name.

She put the mental struggle aside. Figuring out her identity was a different battle for a different day. For the time being, she needed to follow her mother's command to do whatever she had to in order to stay alive.

I will, Mama. I'll make you proud and do what you never were able to.

"The Cordero family is holding a big shindig this coming Saturday night," Rick said quietly at a back table in the bar.

It had become their normal meeting place since Kaden had arrived in Boston. Rick, Kaden, and another detective named Bart had been discussing the best way to infiltrate the compound.

"The invitations say the event is to welcome home Cameron Cordero's long-lost niece," Bart said. "Are you sure she wants to be rescued?"

"Positive," Kaden said. "I snuck onto the property the day after I arrived and saw her with my own eyes. She's being held captive by two goons who don't let her get more than ten feet away from them. So what's the plan? And what do you want me to do?"

"Slow down," Bart said. He stood up and scanned the area. When he was satisfied that no one was within earshot, he resumed his seat. "I have an in with the caterers. They'll get us into the estate. Do you have a tux?"

"I can get one," Kaden said.

"Be ready at five, and I hope you like to serve hors d'oeuvres."

"If it means getting near Frankie, I'll serve anything."

"I have to warn you," Rick said. "One wrong move, and we're dead. There'll be no backup coming to rescue us and no weapons. We're going rogue. The Corderos have people on the force, and if we made this an official operation, they'd know about it. We can't trust anyone. So we have to do it alone, and that means taking risks we wouldn't ordinarily have to."

"I understand and am forever grateful to both of you."

Bart waved away his thanks. "You get your girl, and we get our guy. It's a win-win for all of us. If you need to get hold of us, you know how."

The two men disappeared into the shadows of the bar, leaving Kaden alone to mentally prepare for going behind enemy lines. When he was ready, he found a tux rental place and brought his tux back to the hotel, then braced himself for the long wait until the party.

When Saturday finally arrived, the three men rode onto the estate in one of the vans that belonged to the caterers. Upon their arrival, two big men patted them down. Bart had been right about leaving any weapons at home. As he had said, one wrong move and they would be dead.

"All clear," one of the men said. He smiled at Kaden. "What did you bring for us tonight? I like those little blanket pigs. You got any of those?"

Kaden froze, having no idea what the real caterers planned to serve.

"I asked you a question," the man growled, moving in close.

"We want it to be a surprise," Kaden blurted. "That's all."

The man squinted, considering Kaden's excuse. "I do like surprises. All right, you're good."

The man moved on, and Kaden nearly collapsed at how close he'd come to being kicked out—or worse.

They were ushered into the kitchen and then Kaden was handed a tray of stuffed mushroom caps.

"This is simple," a real server said. "You can't mess it up. You walk around. You hold the tray while you pass them a napkin and a mushroom if they want one. If they don't want it, you keep moving. That's it. If nobody wants anything, you step back and disappear into the walls. But always be on the lookout for anyone who wants something to eat or drink. That's when you are right by their side again. Got it?"

Kaden agreed absently, worrying over how Bart and Rick were faring. They had different tasks and were deep undercover. He had no idea if they'd even gotten in. He prayed things on their end were going smoothly.

Kaden pushed through a set of swinging doors and headed up to the great hall where a group of fewer than fifty people mingled about in their finery. As he made his way through the room, passing out mushroom caps, he searched for the one face he longed to see most.

But Frankie was nowhere to be found.

After he'd made a lap around the room, Kaden stepped back against the wall. He took in all the entrances and thought about going through one of them to search for her.

What if she isn't coming? What if she's hurt?

Cameron Cordero stepped into the room, and the crowd paused to clap and welcome him. He ate up the attention and told some story about a party he'd thrown in prison, which actually sounded more like a country club than a prison from his description.

The guests laughed at all the right places, which made Cameron boast more.

Finally, he said, "But you didn't come here to hear about my antics. You came to meet my precious niece. Francesca Cordero was ripped from our arms and sent to live on a dirt farm as a prisoner her whole life. Now, after twenty-five years, I have found her and brought her home to her rightful place. If my father had lived to see this day, to see his precious granddaughter walk these halls, I know it would have healed the broken heart he died from. I hope I can love her with the same adoration that my father would have. Won't you give my niece a warm welcome home? Everyone, this is my beautiful Francesca." He gestured grandly to the top of the staircase.

Kaden turned with the crowd, and there she was, coming down the stairs in a dress covered in gold jewels and a long train that cascaded down the red-carpeted staircase behind her. She was so regal and fit perfectly in her surroundings, as though she were one of the paintings on the wall.

For a moment, Kaden wondered if she was real.

An elbow nudged his ribs, and he realized the caterer had joined him. "Serve," he commanded under his breath. "Are you trying to blow your cover?"

Kaden snapped to and made his way around the room again. People barely noticed him as they took in the stunning beauty of the young woman who had captured the room. *Oohs* and *aahs* filled the air as people clapped and welcomed her, first from afar, and then up close and personal as she made her way into the crowd. She walked up to her uncle, who kissed both her cheeks and placed her at his right side.

When she faced them all, her smile lit up the room brighter than the jewels on her dress. If Kaden didn't know better, he would think she was loving every minute of the charade. If Rick and Bart were around, he hoped they wouldn't back out of the rescue. Even Kaden had to admit that Frankie appeared comfortable in her surroundings.

Cameron spoke to the crowd as he looped his arm through Frankie's. "I must admit, when my niece arrived home, I didn't think she would be ready to be presented to you all so soon. But she is brilliant and more capable than I ever imagined. Within days, I could see the advantages that her smart mind would bring to my company and to all of you, my clients. You have trusted Cordero Construction through my father's reign, and now ours."

Kaden cringed at his use of the word *reign*. The man thought he was a king. And Frankie was his queen.

The people applauded, and Frankie stepped forward, her smile gracious and warm. "Please, mingle and eat. My uncle has worked hard to bring you the finest delicacies that money can buy. Trust me—I've been going through the books, so I know."

Laughter filtered through the room. Everyone loved her.

Kaden knew the feeling.

He longed to let her know that he was close, to signal that he was going to get her out that night. Slowly, he made his way through the crowd again. From the corner of his eye, he watched her float from guest to guest, shaking hands and charming her uncle's guests.

"It's so nice to have a face to go with the numbers." She lowered her voice to one man and said in a conspiratorial tone, "I happen to know you are one of our biggest clients. Thank you for trusting us with your business."

She approached another man. She offered her hand but remained aloof. "I expect more from you this year. Understood?"

The man's face flooded with red blotches, and he swallowed hard.

"I'm kidding," Frankie said, but there was a hardness in her eyes that belied the words.

People laughed again, but there was an uncomfortable note in it.

Kaden marveled at the new version of the woman he'd fallen in love with. Why was she acting in such a way? It made him feel ill to see her innocence gone. As he stepped closer, he peered into her eyes and noticed that something was different about them. It took every ounce of strength not to drop his tray and haul her from the building. He had to get her out of there before the Frankie he knew was gone forever.

But one slipup, and they were dead.

So Kaden carried his tray, circling around couples and groups until he stood before Frankie. "Mushroom cap?"

Their gazes locked. For a mere second, her eyes widened, and she reached a hand to her slender neck. "No thank you. Go away."

A few people close by inhaled sharply, and Cameron stepped up beside his niece. "My precious, is there a problem? Is this man bothering you?"

"Not at all. I don't like mushrooms," she said archly. "They make me sick. I want him to take them out of here. Right now."

"Of course, my darling." He faced Kaden. "You heard her. Get the mushrooms out of here, and don't bring them back again." Cameron beamed at the crowd. "We still have so much to learn about each other after the years we lost together, but I love getting to know my niece. Note to self—no mushrooms in the future."

The crowd laughed, a touch nervously.

Kaden had no choice but to leave the ballroom. He was shocked that Frankie had sent him away. Did she think she was protecting him? Did she doubt that he could take care of her? After all, he'd failed her on his first day as her protector. The probability of that being the truth cut deep. But after losing her in Idaho, he deserved her distrust of him.

The other reason he thought of made his blood run cold. What if Frankie had become a true Cordero? Whether they'd brainwashed her, or she'd succumbed willingly, Kaden had to consider that the Frankie he knew might not exist anymore.

He set down the tray and stood against a curtain. He didn't dare return to the kitchen. Anything could happen, and he needed to be there to jump in, whether she wanted his protection or not.

Cameron stood at the front of the room, addressing the crowd once again. "I'd like to deal with the business side of things first, and then we can continue with our celebration. Please welcome Francesca to the podium for a few words."

Frankie glided to the podium and lowered the mic. "Thank you all for coming. As I said earlier, I feel like I know you already. But as I was familiarizing myself with your companies in my uncle's books,

I noted a few business things to discuss that I thought would be better addressed to you as a whole, rather than individually. Thank you, Uncle Cam, for allowing me this time."

She faced the crowd again and said, "First, I want to assure you that all your businesses are safe and will continue with the Cordero family. So you can all let out a collective sigh of relief."

Laughter filtered through the room again. Some even released that sigh of relief. Frankie was good. Really good. Again, Kaden wondered if she was becoming one of them after all. If she had, that meant it was likely she would tell her uncle who he was. He realized she held his life in her hands. But he had to believe she wouldn't send him to his death. Not after everything they'd been through.

"There is one small discrepancy that I have found in the books that I would like to bring to everyone's attention."

The room dropped to dead silence.

"It appears that someone in the room is stealing from us."

People stared at each other, obviously questioning whether she was referring to them. Men tugged at their collars as if they were too warm. Women paled beneath their elaborate makeup.

Cameron stepped up to the podium, his brow furrowed. "Francesca, what is this about?"

"Uncle, I think you need to know that this man"—she pointed to a man with white hair and a goatee—"has been stealing from you, and I can prove it."

Cameron gaped at the man. "You have been doing business with us for decades, both with me and with my father before me. Is this true? Are you stealing from me?"

"Of course not," he protested, but Kaden wasn't convinced, and by the expressions around him, neither was anyone else. "I have always done business with Cordero construction because I respect this company.

She's lying. Why would you believe her over your trusted clients?"

"You're right. Everyone please calm down," Cameron said, obviously trying to keep the peace. "Francesca, I'm putting a stop to this right now."

"But don't you want the truth to be revealed? Don't you want to know who is honest and who is a thief? For example, you, Mr. Shaw. Did you know that Cameron is stealing from you?"

"Excuse me?" Mr. Shaw shouted.

"That is enough, Francesca." Cameron advanced toward her.

Kaden did as well, though he knew Cameron would get to her first.

Frankie continued at the podium. "Mr. Sterling, Cameron has been stealing from you since his release as well."

"That's it!" Cameron launched himself at his niece, reaching for her throat.

The windows shattered as police officers swung in on ropes. The crowd screamed and scattered in every direction as Cameron's men drew their weapons to fire on the invaders. But the police had been prepared for that, and they safely apprehended the Cordero thugs.

Kaden wondered where the police had come from. Rick and Bart had said there would be no backup. Then he saw Frankie smiling as two officers dragged her uncle off of her. Kaden realized she'd orchestrated the whole thing. The police had been lying in wait on the roof because of her. Everything he'd seen that night had been her playing a part until she could divide Cameron from his associates and take him down.

She'd used her mind and her gift with numbers to destroy the man who would have owned her for life.

Suddenly, Cameron broke free of the officers and snatched a gun from his tux coat. He leveled it at Frankie, mere feet away, and pulled the trigger. The blast wrenched through the air, and Kaden watched her fall backward as if in slow motion, yet he had no time to get to her before the bullet did. One moment she was standing, and the next she was down on the ground.

Yet so was Cameron. But how?

Even as he ran through the ballroom, Kaden peered around until he spotted Frankie's father, holding a rifle on the other side of the chaos-packed room. Chris, or rather Daniel, had once been a sharpshooter, and he'd used his skill to save his daughter's life.

Or so Kaden hoped.

He finally reached the podium and fell to his knees beside Frankie. Her arm was covered in blood, but the bullet had barely grazed her.

He scooped her up and held her close, whispering prayers of gratitude.

"Kaden, I was so scared when I saw you," she said, reaching a hand to his cheek. "They could have killed you."

"I'm okay. And you will be too," he assured her.

She clung to his hand. "I want to go home. I want to go back to my farm."

"And you will. I promise. I will find a way. It's where you belong. I'll take you there myself."

She shook her head. "No. I want you to go after your dreams in Alaska."

"Oh, Frankie. *You* are my dream."

"You want a life of adventure. I don't. You have to go, or you'll always regret it."

The paramedics swept in and lifted Frankie from his arms. As they strapped her to a stretcher, she called out one more time. "Go to your beautiful Alaska. I know what it feels like to be in a prison. I know the life you've had under your father's thumb. Let me love you the best way I know how—by giving you your freedom. Be free, Kaden."

With that, the paramedics whisked her away, leaving Kaden to contemplate her words. But all he could think was that a life without Frankie felt like the real prison. How could he convince her that her love already set him free?

As Kaden made his way outside, the two men that Frankie had called out during her speech ran up to him. They peeled off their facial hair, revealing Rick and Bart wearing huge grins.

"Nice work, buddy," Rick said. "The Cordero dynasty is done."

Kaden sought both their faces. "Wait, did you know she was going to call you out?"

"Of course. We had it all worked out, but we couldn't tell you. The one thing we hadn't planned on was the sniper."

Would the police go after Frankie's father? "He saved her life."

"He got away. I didn't get a good look at him. Did you?" Bart asked Rick.

"Nope. Must've been someone Cameron ripped off. It seems Cameron stole from the wrong person this time and paid with his life. But what about your girl? Now that she's free, what's the plan?"

Kaden smiled. "Now I convince her to marry me."

Frankie knew she had told Kaden to follow his dreams, but she had never suspected he would leave right away. By the time she left the hospital, he had flown out of Boston without so much as a goodbye.

Maybe that's for the best, she thought, trying to ignore the wound in her heart. *No sense waiting to wipe the slate clean.*

She decided to do some moving of her own. When she landed in Seattle, two men from the U.S. Marshals were waiting for her, ready to take her into the program again.

"I'm going home," she told them. "Give me back my old identity and let me live my life."

"You could still be in danger. There is a chance Cameron had someone coming up behind him to take over," an agent explained.

"Yeah, it was me. There was no one else. Trust me—I had access to all his secret books. He scared so many people, and they're happy he's gone."

After much arguing and then investigating the situation themselves, the men eventually approved her return to Nighthawk Farm with her name intact. She was actually surprised that they were so accommodating. They said her father had purchased the land from the government over the years, and it was hers free and clear if going back was her choice. All Frankie knew was that she would never let anyone lock her up behind brick walls again. She supposed there was a chance someone would want to make the heir to the Cordero fortune go away permanently, but that wasn't her. It was Vera. And Frankie knew her mother could handle herself.

When Frankie stepped up onto her porch, back at her farm, she took a few minutes to survey her land. Hers. She was finally home.

She grabbed a broom and began cleaning up from the night they'd run for their lives, delighting in the work. Shards of glass crunched beneath her shoes as she swept them into a pile. She'd already checked the pasture and barn and found her animals gone, either out in the wild or in government custody. She added figuring out which to her list of things to do. She would also check on what had happened to Greg's animals. If she had to replace them, it would be a while before she could afford more horses, but she had all the time in the world. After the breakneck pace of the last month, she was happy to work toward her own little goals.

When the porch met with her satisfaction, she went inside and cleaned the mess left when her father took the bullet that had nearly killed her. *Well*, she amended. *The first bullet that nearly killed me.* Her arm was still tender from the second. It felt like years ago, but in actuality had barely been a few weeks. The place felt strange without her father, but not necessarily wrong. She supposed he had been preparing her for that day her whole life.

She walked to his room and found everything as he'd left it. Even the bags he had packed to run away were still on his dresser. She hoped he was safe and alive out there somewhere.

"I miss you, Papa. But I'm taking your room." She smiled. "Not today, though. Today, I have a farm to tend to."

There was so much work to do. Frankie changed into her overalls and boots and set out to tackle it. Fences had blown over, fruit needed harvesting, and it was long past time to bring her business into the current century. She loved her father for protecting her, but those days were over. Nighthawk Farm would be a contender, offering the best apples that side of the Mississippi River.

Her third day on the farm, Frankie sat back on her porch swing to watch the sunset over the mountains, sipping a glass of iced tea and reveling in her newfound peace.

She heard the crunch of gravel before she saw a car coming down the lane.

It was a black car, like the ones Cameron's men drove.

Frankie felt her heart in her throat and stood to run. Had the U.S. Marshals been right about someone tracking her down to kill her?

The car came to a stop, and a young man climbed out. "Miss Frankie Stiles?"

"Who wants to know?" she asked cautiously, reaching for a shotgun by the front door. She'd kept it nearby since her return, just in case.

The man put up his hands to show he was unarmed. "I didn't mean to startle you. I'm an attorney. I have a sealed letter from a woman named Vera Cordero. May I give it to you?"

Frankie hiked up the gun to show she would use it if he tried anything. "Leave it on the bottom step."

The man did as she said, then retreated so she could pick it up. She bent to grab it and tucked the rifle under her arm so she could unseal the envelope. Inside was a letter.

Dear Frankie,

If you're reading this, then you made it out alive. I knew you could do it. I held the men off as long as I could. Once they realized you weren't with me, they raced back to Boise to find you. I had hoped you would be long gone, but in the end, you succeeded in doing what I never could. The world is a safer place because of you.

However, it's still not safe for me. I've made a lot of enemies through the years, working for my father. For this reason, I have decided to go into witness protection. It's something I wish I had done twenty-five years ago with you and your father, but I wasn't brave enough yet. You taught me that it could be done, and that I wouldn't lose my identity with a name change.

So, my darling daughter, I can't say I will see you again, but I also can't say I won't. I need you to know I'm not alone. Your papa says hi, and that he loves you so much. We respect your decision not to return to the program and wish you all the best.

We also have a gift for you. The man who gave you this letter will now give you another envelope. Your father says to go put your farm on the map, once and for all.

Until we meet again, my beloved, fearless girl, whether this side of heaven or not.

Love,

Papa and Mama

Frankie swiped at tears running down her cheeks. Her parents were together, reuniting after twenty-five years, until death parted them.

"She says you have something else for me?" she asked the lawyer.

"Yes." He held out another envelope. "I'm supposed to read this one aloud."

"Okay." She waited as he opened it.

He shook the paper as off in the distance a loud noise reverberated around them. He raised his voice over the sound. "I hereby decree that full ownership of Nighthawk Farm belongs to Francesca Stiles. Along with the land itself, she acquires all buildings on the property—ten horses, four cows, and a helicopter."

The motor from above grew louder, and she realized it was landing.

"A helicopter? What was Papa thinking? I can't fly that thing."

"I'm not finished," the man shouted over the sound, his blond hair whipping in the wind. "She also acquires the love of one man named Kaden Phillips. This one is up to Frankie, however. Should she decide to reject the offer, the aforementioned Mr. Phillips promises to be a nuisance to his neighbor until she agrees to marry him."

"Neighbor? Let me see that. What do you mean by neighbor? And what do you mean by marry?" She stepped down to the ground to snatch the letter, but before she reached the lawyer, Kaden jumped out of the helicopter and ran in her direction under the spinning blades.

"What on earth are you up to?" she shouted at him. "You're supposed to be flying over Alaska right now."

He stopped a foot away from her and dropped to one knee. He removed a black box from his pocket and opened it to reveal a beautiful diamond ring.

"Frankie," he began. "When I left Idaho to fly to Alaska, I believed I was going to find a new home. But something bigger than me knew this farm was my home—that *you* were my home. I don't need to keep searching when all I want is standing right in front of me. I know you thought you were setting me free by making me go, but I'm not free unless I'm with you. Any other place will keep me locked out of a life with you. Could you really sentence me to such a place?"

Frankie rolled her eyes to the skies. "You're being ridiculous."

He smiled brightly up at her. "I'm a desperate man. Desperately in love, and desperate to start a life with you on this farm. What do you say? I have to warn you, if you say no, I'll be relentless. I'll be over here every day to ask you again and again until you finally let me put this ring on your finger."

"That could get really annoying. You're starting to sound like Greg."

"I understand how he felt, to live next door to you yet be forced to love you from afar. I'm begging you to put me out of my misery and say yes."

"What do you mean, live next door to me?"

"I sold my plane and used it as a down payment for Greg's ranch. I mean to honor the man who wanted to help you and keep his ranch alive. I can do both of those things."

"Kaden, that's sweet."

"Sweet enough to say yes?"

"You really mean to take over where Greg left off." She glanced toward the ranch. Greg's fate would hurt her heart forever. He hadn't deserved to be gunned down, even if he had wanted her for her land rather than for love. "It does feel right to care for his property as our own."

"And it would belong to both of us, as husband and wife."

"Until death do us part?"

"Forever and ever."

"My parents are together again," she said.

Kaden stood and wrapped an arm around her waist to pull her close, the ring between them. "I know. They contacted me before I left Boston. They told me you might go back into the program as well, and asked what I planned to do if you did."

"What did you say?" she asked.

"I said if you went back in, then I would go with you. We were all waiting for your decision." He smiled quickly. "You gave those Marshals such a hard time. They came back to the office and said no one would mess with you anyway."

"You were there?"

"Sweetheart, I was waiting for you. We all were."

Tears filled her eyes at what he was saying. "You would have gone into witness protection and left everything behind for me?"

He cupped her face in his hands. "Frankie, I don't know how else to say this to you. You are my home. Wherever you are is where I will go. How can I make you understand?"

A cry escaped her lips, and she flung her arms around his neck.

Kaden lifted her off the ground. "Is that a yes?"

"Yes!" Frankie held out her hand for him to slide the ring on her finger. "It's beautiful."

"You're beautiful." He kissed her sweetly on the lips. "How about a ride in my helicopter?"

"I would love that."

They headed toward the aircraft, but soon realized the attorney was still there, holding the letter.

"I'm sorry, is there more?" Frankie asked him.

"I'm afraid so, but I'll try not to hold you up much longer." He cleared his throat. "In addition to the items I've mentioned, Miss Stiles will also receive the trust fund that was created for her at birth under the name Francesca Paparella, in the current sum of two million dollars. And not to worry. This fund was started with legal money and not part of the seized Cordero assets. It was a fund started by your parents and has grown exponentially due to Vera's investment skills."

Frankie gawked at him, unable to speak.

The man handed the letter to her. "Everything you need to claim your funds is in the letter. All the best to you." He returned to his car, then paused with his hand on the door. "You are a wealthy young lady, Miss Stiles."

Frankie nodded and leaned her head against Kaden's chest. "I am rich beyond measure, sir, and it has nothing to do with money."

As they watched the lawyer drive off, Kaden guided her toward the helicopter and started to laugh.

"What's so funny?"

Kaden had tears of laughter in his eyes as he said, "Wait until my father hears I married the farmer's daughter." He laughed even harder, causing Frankie to join him in his joyful victory over the man who thought he owned Kaden.

As they rose in the helicopter, Frankie caught sight of her land below, while her future husband flew free through the skies.

They had made it work after all.

She reached for Kaden's hand, and together they set out for the bright future before them. It was sure to be clear skies.